ROBAK'S RUN

ROBAK'S RUN

JOE L. HENSLEY

A CRIME CLUB BOOK
DOUBLEDAY
NEW YORK LONDON TORONTO SYDNEY AUCKLAND

A Crime Club Book
PUBLISHED BY DOUBLEDAY
a division of
Bantam Doubleday Dell Publishing Group, Inc.
666 Fifth Avenue, New York, New York 10103

DOUBLEDAY and the portrayal of a man
with a gun are trademarks of
Doubleday, a division of Bantam Doubleday Dell
Publishing Group, Inc.

Library of Congress Cataloging-in-Publication Data

Hensley, Joe L., 1926–
    Robak's run / Joe L. Hensley.—1st ed.
        p.   cm.
    "A Crime club book."
    I. Title.
PS3558.E55R68   1990
813'.54—dc20   89-38525
                                                        CIP
                    ISBN 0-385-26700-2
            Copyright © 1990 by Joe L. Hensley

ROBAK'S RUN

ONE

"Steinmetz's Memoirs" (manuscript) page 43: "The moving finger writes and having writ leaves admissible evidence behind."

VERY EARLY that Wednesday morning I ran my normal path along the Ohio River, five miles, part in town and part of it past the city limits. It was a good place to run. I had half a dozen paths I used at times, but I liked this one best. During the run I could smell the river odors mixed in with Maytime greenery and flowers. I could see the old houses, some of them fine mansions, some of them shacks, that lay above (and some also within) the flood zone of the river. I ran and I was content.

Later that morning, after a shower and shave and Spartan breakfast, about eight, I went to the county jail to see my latest client, Stanley "Stan the Man" Willetts, who was accused of doing in his wife Honey (true name: Ruby Geneva) with a sledge hammer in the midst of an argument about her extramarital affairs. I'd been appointed for him late the day before by an apologetic Judge Harner.

"You're the only attorney in town with extensive experience in murder cases," he'd told me in his soft voice. He'd looked around his deserted circuit courtroom and nodded to himself, perhaps remembering another rea-

son why I was his man of the moment. "And this fellow
Willetts asked specifically for you, even demanded you,
when I inquired if he wanted a lawyer to represent him.
I know that his demands don't mean anything legally
and I know I don't have to appoint the attorney a penni-
less defendant wants, but Willetts said, in open court
and right on the record, that he didn't do it, despite all
the damning circumstantial evidence I'd heard in a
probable cause hearing. And he also seemed to think
that part of the reason he was in jail was because his
deceased wife's mother, Mildred Standish, is the vice-
chairman of my political party." He looked around his
hot courtroom again and lifted a black-robed arm and
wiped his forehead. "So would you please take the case
and take care of several knotty, if not insoluble, problems for me? If there's anything I don't need it's someone running around the jail or around town saying I do
things politically."

He was a decent judge, ten years younger than me,
trying hard at his job, and I liked him a lot, even if once,
four plus years back now, he'd defeated my close friend
Judge Steinmetz in Steinmetz's last reelection try, and
even if he was slightly caught up in the web of his own
importance. Judges are judges and they are important,
but lawyers believe they must not show it. The rest of
us in the law learn to live with judges and their importance, but not with any outward showing of that importance. What we want is a Solomon on our side.

I thought about his request for a moment. I didn't
need or want added work. There was plenty to do. And
I was senior enough in the local pecking order that I
probably could just say no.

I sighed and didn't. "Sure, Your Honor. I've read a
little about the case in the local paper and it sounded

hopeless, but I'll do it. I didn't know that the dead wife was the daughter of one of our area's politicians, but it doesn't bother me. I know Mildred Standish. My bet is she doesn't much like me. Can I get copies of what's in the court file? And a transcript of the probable cause hearing if it's been typed?"

He handed me a sheaf of papers. "I had the court reporter make copies of what's in the file. And she's working on the transcript. We'll get you a copy of that as soon as it's completed. That should be within a few days. Lots of people heard him threaten her, lots of people saw them fighting. And there's a state technician's positive make on fingerprints on the weapon." He sighed. "Maybe we'll be rewarded and this one will be a short trial or, better, a plead out."

At eight in the morning in late spring the whole world of Bington is lovely. The old brick buildings imperfectly but charmingly reflect the early morning sun. One can forget that the plumbing inside the old beauties the local fanatical preservationists dote on is corroded and clogged. One can disremember that the wiring is threadbare and bad enough to be a substantial fire hazard for the local volunteers. One can ignore the fact that a brisk wind could fold in many a handsome, bulging ivy brick wall.

At eight in the morning even Mojeff's county jail looks fine and lovely. Someone intelligent and farseeing, years ago, had decided that a new jail should look like the rest of the town, and so it had come to pass that way thanks to county commissioners and county council. The jail, now twenty years old, looks to be a hundred plus. It looks, on the outside, just as if it were constructed of old bricks and vines. It looks like anyone with a can opener could break out. But prisoners seldom do because inside the jail it is modern.

I opened a pair of doors and an alarm on the wall announced me. Sheriff Goldie sat behind his desk and drank coffee from a cup big enough to hide his generous mouth as he watched me come in. Deputies and trustees carried tin trays and served a bountiful breakfast of fried doughnuts and coffee to the caged. The interior of the jail smelled of that coffee mixed with garbage and diluted with just a touch of early morning urine.

"I heared you drawed Stan the Man," Goldie said, grinning impishly up at me from his swivel chair.

"Another innocent victim of brutal police oppression," I said. "And I've also heard that one of our local leaders is seeking revenge against him."

Sheriff Goldie leaned back in his chair and took a large bite out of his doughnut. He was a good man and a decent enough sheriff, not bright, not dumb, popular with the courthouse wall crowd, and a man with a lot of relatives here, there, and everywhere in Bington and Mojeff County. I'd made him look good a time or two and he, like me, had little use for Herman Leaks, Bington's longtime prosecutor. I'd also heard that his opposition in the last primary election had owned the help of his local party leaders. I could almost see him adding and subtracting and coming to early solutions in my favor.

"It ain't visitin' hours just now, but you want to see him?"

"Yes, but it can wait until you finish breakfast."

He glanced down at the doughnut and the steaming coffee as if surprised they were there. "I finished breakfast a hour ago. Sausage patties, eggs, and biscuits with sawmill gravy. This here's just to tide me over some until early lunch." He got up in good humor. "Stanley ain't over-happy with us or the state troopers, Don. Usually when we catch him he does a quick two and a half with twist off the low board into the prosecutor's plea-bargain. You ask him what his profession is and he'll admit, kind of proud-like, that he's a burglar." He shook his head. "Ain't that easy this time. It's murder and some in the town out there's heated up because Stan got out on early parole and then come right home and killed his little wife, Honey, in a mean and ugly style." He looked me in the eye. "Wasn't much left of her face. If you want I could show you pictures. One blow and she was dead, but the perp took a lot more smacks at her." He waited for me to ask about the pictures and, when I didn't, he went on. "Now Stanley is screaming he didn't kill her. My guess is that he did. The victim's mother would like to turn it into a public hanging with her handling the final rope. And maybe she will. Odd, because she and the daughter had little use for each other until Mildred won some lottery money."

"What have you got for evidence?"

"Stanley was seen at her house almost all day the day she was done in. We got some letters he wrote her from prison saying he'd be awful mad if she'd taken up with anyone else and that he'd already heard she had. Some neighbors listened to him threaten her, lots of neighbors. Then the state boys said his fingerprints were on the sledge hammer. He claims it was from using the hammer to do some work for her."

"Where are they on the sledge hammer?"

"All over the handle. He run like a deer when us and the locals and the state cops staked out the riverfront and went to catch him." He gave me a wise look. "But

maybe with you in it I'd bet the prosecutor, Herm the
Germ, would go for voluntary manslaughter if you
could talk sense into Stan. I mean Stan, he's spent a lot
of his life in reform schools, work camps, and prisons.
Once he was outside and free for two whole years
straight and that's when he married Mildred Standish's
daughter. How well are you acquainted with Mildred?"

"I know her is all."

"Well then you also know how she do go on. But it
ain't like being here in jail or in prison's a world Stan
don't know or that he was a brand new jailhouse
cherry." He patted me on the shoulder in comradely
fashion. "You talk to him, Don. He's heard some big
crap about you from one of the jail lawyers and he
thinks you can wish him out of here. Once he finds out
you can't, he'll change his story and things will ease out.
And I don't think Boss Mildred can change Herm the
Germ's mind on a decent plea-bargain because he don't
like her no better than I do. Something biting on that
woman. She cried and went on fierce."

"I'll sure give Stanley a try, Goldie."

He nodded, believing me. He lived in a reasonable
world. "Follow me. We got him all alone in a single cell
just like he was important or dangerous or somethin'.
You mind me putting you in the cell with him and leaving the two of you to talk?"

I knew a little about "Stan the Man." One of the reasons he was called by the nickname was because he was
small in size. His life had been a series of thefts, bad
checks, and burglaries. He was a modestly skilled burglar who went for stores, not homes. He was not re-
puted ever to have been a strong-arm robber, but was
known rather as a man who stole for a living, and who
was reasonably competent at it.

"Cell's okay, Sheriff. We can talk there."

I followed behind Goldie. We entered the cell area. In a large holding area, barred and locked, the morning crew awaited going to county and/or circuit court. They were a motley group, seven in number, ready to face the judge and the judge's hereafters on this early Wednesday morning.

"Three DUI's, a wife-beater, two druggies, and a shoplifter," Goldie said over his shoulder. "A quiet night. You want any of them?"

"No," I said, smiling, but only a little. *When I'd been younger and hungrier there'd been a time.*

One of the prisoners called out to me. "No one read me no rights, Robak. And I ain't even got to make my constitutional phone call." He let out a stream of professional cursing and Goldie and I listened to him politely.

"Shut up, Whitedog," Goldie said amiably when he paused for breath. "When they brought you in you was too drunk to hear your Mirandas and too sick to use the phone."

We walked past the holding tank and on down the corridor. There were two empty cells and then, around a corner, we came upon Stanley Willetts. He sat huddled against the wall on a cot, glowering out at the world. He had a blanket pulled tight around him although the interior of the jail was warm enough to be uncomfortable for me.

"I'm Don Robak," I said at the cell door.

Stanley Willetts nodded. "I know who you are, Mr. Robak," he said. He smiled at me revealing good teeth. He got up and thrust his hand through an opening in the cell. The hand that shook mine was cool, but of medium strength. "I wasn't sure you'd bother taking my case."

Sheriff Goldie opened the door and admitted me to
the cell. "You men can talk. I'll be back here in fifteen or
twenty minutes, Don. Is that enough time?"

"Plenty for now," I said.

I sat down on the far edge of the cell cot and Willetts
and I watched Goldie relock and go jingling back down
the corridor.

"I sure thank you for coming over to try helping me,
Mr. Robak," Willetts said.

I looked him over, somewhat impressed. I decided he
was around forty years old. He was thin and his face
was pinched and tired, but he was not ugly. He wore a
narrow, dapper mustache and had a full head of brown,
curly hair. He was built well and his handshake had
shown me he had some strength. I knew, from other
burglars I'd represented, that safe men were medium
strong. They had to be to peel back the layers of steel on
the safes they burgled. But if I put a suit on this guy and
had him read a Bible in court and cry into his handkerchief when he talked about how someone had killed his
lovely, dear wife, plus if I could figure a way to muffle
the testimony of the victim's mother, then maybe, just
maybe . . .

"The sheriff and the judge told me you were arrested
this time for beating your wife, Honey, to death with a
sledge hammer. The sheriff also told me the prosecutor
wants a heavy piece of your butt. Maybe that's partly on
account of your mother-in-law and her place in the local
sun, but I'm told that the prosecutor might go light if
you cooperate. You'd have to admit in court you killed
your wife in a rage. Probably get twenty and do ten of
it. In a trial you might get a lot more if we lost. Forty to
sixty years." I watched him as I talked. Nothing in his
face changed. "Is that what happened, Mr. Willetts? Did

you get angry at your wife and kill her in a jealous rage?"

"No. No sir. I was pretty mad at her because I knew she was running around on me when I was in prison. But she'd done that lots before and I'd let it go and we'd gotten back together. This time I came home and she didn't want to get back together. She wouldn't let me move in, but she did let me come around the house and work on it for her. I was good enough to do that. And one time I thought maybe we was going to get back together."

"One time?"

He smiled. "One time only and I messed that up. The house stuff was new and expensive and I asked her about that when I was in bed with her and we was done. She got mad and said I'd never trusted her and that all I was and would ever be was a jailbird. Then I got mad and I threatened her again and I guess the neighbors heard. The houses out there is close together and the neighbors are nosy."

"What happened then?"

"She went instant from loving to mad and she run me off and told me not to come back or she'd call the law. She said her bitch mother, who hates me, had told her to get a divorce and that she'd give Honey the money to file it so Honey wouldn't have to use hers." He looked at the wall and then back at me. "But she was all there was for me so I kept coming back after that and talking nice and she kept running me off. She wasn't workin' much anywhere and here was all this new stuff in her house. New furniture, new pictures, lots of canned food on the shelves. Someone told me her mother won a lottery, but I couldn't see her giving any to Honey. I watched the house nights trying to see who it was backdooring me, and if it was one man only, but I never saw anything or anyone. Funny."

"Were you around the night she was killed?"

"For a while. Early. She run me off, said again I had to leave or she'd call the law. She let me work all day and then run me off. There's a place I'd go, down on the river. A shack. Bums sleep there. I slept there because she'd not let me sleep at the house. No one saw me there. No one else slept there, it being cool. I stayed there all night. That shack is where they caught me."

"But you didn't kill her?"

"No sir. I swear it on my father's grave, Mr. Robak." He thought about it and gave me a look full of futility and anger. "Someone did her in and made it look like it was me that done it. They did her in mean and nasty." He frowned like a country parson hearing a four letter word. "I didn't do it."

I'd heard the song before and I no longer automatically believed.

Stanley Willetts read my doubting look and lost eye contact with me. He looked down at the floor and I followed his eyes. We watched two spiders moving quickly around each other in mysterious spring rites. Maybe they sensed us watching because one went up a cell bar and the other hid behind the toilet.

"You know my mother-in-law, Mildred?" he asked, soft-voiced.

"I know who she is, but I belong to the other party, if you're getting sudden doubts," I said, smiling, but only a little.

Willetts knotted his hands and curbed his suspicions of me for the moment. "They say in here that you're good at digging into cases like mine, political kind of cases—I mean where a man's accused, they're hot after him, and he ain't guilty. I heard some guys in here talking about you and I asked questions. They told me the prosecutor don't much like you, but then he don't much like me either. I know I've been in lots of trouble before, but this time I didn't do it. Will you look at it and try to help me, Mr. Robak?"

"I'll do what I can," I said.

"Someone beat my Honey to death, Mr. Robak. They used a sledge hammer I'd used working earlier and they used it on her a lot. You ask around. Folks will tell you I ain't a vicious man. I steal things. It's my profession and what I do. But this time maybe I could be real bad to whoever done Honey in. Like they was to her. Mean." He looked out of the bars and then back at me. "It don't make no sense at all. She didn't have a new man, but she did have all this nice stuff. And I watched to see and no one came."

"When's she supposed to have been killed?"

"Late Friday night or early Saturday morning. Sheriff, when he questioned me, said somewhere after eleven and before one. I worked on the house for her most of the day on Friday afternoon before we got into it again. I was chipping at paint, getting ready to paint the outside of the house. I used the sledge hammer early that day to break up some stones that bordered her garden, get them down to near the size of the others already there. She asked me to do it. I left the sledge hammer outside near the porch. Mostly, that day, I just chipped paint." He shook his head. "She kept the inside of her old house pretty and neat." He shook his head. "It had lots of new stuff and, when I first come home, I thought it was for me, a homecoming, a yellow ribbon. I hoped maybe she'd been working, but she hadn't a lot. And she ain't got no money and her mother never had any

either. Lotto, Blotto. But Honey wouldn't even kiss me
that first day, and she kept bawlin' when I'd ask. She
was afraid I'd break something in the house. She never
let me move in. And we never made love except that
one time when maybe the heat got her." He shook his
head unbelievingly. "Honey, she liked making love, but
she cried about it that day. It was like she wanted me,
but didn't want me. Someone . . ."

"Do you know whether anything was taken out of
her house?"

"I saw some things when I was inside, but I never
was inside after she was found dead."

"I'll check." I got up. I'd heard Sheriff Goldie coming
down the corridor. "Anyone wants to talk to you anymore you tell them you'll only talk with me present.
Understand?"

Willetts nodded and stood up with me. He was half a
head shorter than I was. He offered me his hand again
and we shook.

"Thanks," he said.

"I'll be back sometime soon."

My next stop was Herman Leaks and his prosecutor's
office. These days I always like to personally inform
Herman, first thing, that I'm in a case. The reason for
this is that he views me with a substantial amount of
well-nurtured hate. I've had some luck against him. So,
once he knows I'm in a case, we can both start figuring
ways to work things out so that he need not try the case.
Most people charged with crime are guilty and I'm not
above taking advantage of the fact that I've won some to
get an advantage for my client in a plea-bargain. It's
what I'm paid for, like it or not. It's the Democratic
(and Republican) way. Plea-bargains are now a fact of

life in the U.S. of A. The candidate for prosecutor who claims he won't plea-bargain will soon be knee deep in doo-doo, with a jail full of people awaiting trial, and an angry crowd around the jail.

I was conducted to Herman's office by a new receptionist. This one was very young and dewey, sweet-featured and intent, impressed with her job and with Herman. She waited at his door, watching me suspiciously until Herman waved her away.

"Where do you find them like that?" I asked curiously.

"Just finished her first year in law school," Herman said. "Full of fire and resolve and high ideals. She believes working in my office as a gofer will look good on her resume when she gets out into the real world and wants a job." He smiled without meaning and touched a finger to his neat, small mustache. "I hear you got appointed for Stan the Man. I got me a strong circumstantial case against him, but I don't have any eyeball witnesses. I'd maybe deal him for something less than murder."

"And why would you do that, Herm? It seems to me that you could be under some pressure not to deal in this one."

He shrugged. "You mean Mildred Standish? I am, I guess, but I'm weathering it. She doesn't run this office." He nodded to himself. "Confidentially I'm looking forward to thwarting her and ruining her revenge day."

We eyed each other, keeping up the fiction that we were friends and toilers together in a justice system that creaks and groans, where single-issue groups and single-issue people cry for blood for selling drugs or drinking/driving or business crimes or child abuse, and more time and money is spent on whether or not abortions should be permitted than any other issue except the eternal, unending criminal appeals.

"What do you want?"

"I'd settle for voluntary."

"I hope I can do that, Herman. Stanley's told me that he didn't do it and he wanted me to check a few things. I'll quietly check them out and then get back to you. I promised him I'd take a good look. And one of the people I feel like I ought to check out is Mildred Standish."

He smiled maliciously. "That's okay. I might even loan you Stan's hammer from the state police evidence room."

"And I need to check out other people, too," I added.

Herman shook his head sadly. "Robak, you're the eighth wonder of the world. This guy gets paroled out of prison, fights with his wife, and then kills her with a heavy hammer. We got threats heard and threats he admits making. We got witnesses who saw him around her house raising hell. We got a big hammer with his prints and her blood on it. He's ripe meat if you try it."

"How about his clothes? Was any of her blood on his clothes?"

"We think he washed off good in the river. He had plenty of time. The body wasn't found until late morning the next day."

"Was anything missing from the house?"

"I don't know. Out there where she lives they do steal things."

"Where'd she get the new stuff in the house and shelves full of canned goods?"

"Ask her mother. I heard some lottery money came in a couple of months back and that she shared it with Honey."

"Stan says she was running around on him at times before, while he was in prison. Someone, maybe someone other than her mother, was supporting her—because he says she didn't have any kind of steady job. Do you know who she was running around with?"

"No. I do have a statement from the defendant that says she usually ran around when he was in prison. My opinion is this time he decided to do something mean on it."

"I promise you I don't want to try the case," I said humbly. "But I do want to check it some. He's in jail, so he's already doing time. And what I find out in doing the checking I'll bring here first."

"Promise?" he asked. "No newspapers, no television or radio, no surprises in or out of court?" *I'd done all those things to him before and I was unrepentant about them.*

"I promise. And in return I want your promise to me that you won't fold to pressure from Mildred Standish."

"That's easy. Mildred got into party work hoping to make big dollars on it. She hasn't, what with us losing the state election, so she's unhappy. Then she won a lottery wad. Some say it was a million, but I heard it was fifty thousand."

"I'd like to know for sure."

"Me also. My source is probably right. Fifty thousand. Pretty good money. Found money. When Mildred was in here she said she set it up so the lottery people were paying half to her and half to Honey. Could be."

"Let me check."

"Your job's to talk some sense to Stanley Willetts. Just because his wife ran around on him doesn't mean he can beat her face flat with a sledge hammer. That's against the law, Robak. It's murder if we go to trial, voluntary if he pleads. A lot of years' difference in time served by your client." His face was a little red. It always got that way when he made a speech. I could count on it when he summed up to a jury. I'd always warn the jury about it in *voir dire.*

"I promise you I'll try hard, Herman. Can I get copies of what's in your file and your list of witnesses?"

He waved a tired, negligent hand, dismissing me. "Sure, sure. You can have it all. It's a dead cinch kind of case." He laughed. "It's like the old joke where you leave your girl in the car and tell her you're going into a drugstore for rubbers and when you come back she's still there sitting on the front seat and smiling. A dead cinch." He shook his head dolefully. "Only these days the girl would have herpes."

I laughed dutifully. I remembered the joke from my dim boyhood.

In a few moments I did have copies of all his file.

I put the prosecutor's stuff, along with the rest of the papers I'd gotten in court, in a Manila folder file I was carrying. I'd printed Stanley Willetts's name on the tab.

I said good-by to the young lady who was gofering for Herman. She gave me a hard look that let me know she'd remember me and get me for my involvement with common criminals one day when she was in charge of Bington's world.

I left.

I went back up the alley toward the office. A police car pulled over and rolled the window down. A man in blue with a serious look on his face beckoned me over to the car.

And I heard the bad news about Steinmetz.

TWO

"Steinmetz's Memoirs" *(manuscript) page 103: "The thing about hospitals is that people die there."*

As I'VE GROWN OLDER I've also discovered I like visiting hospitals less.

But Steinmetz was inside this hospital as the police had reported to me. I'd called Doctor Hugo Buckner and he'd ordered me to come to the hospital forthwith.

The Bington Hospital was out near the university. I drove past anxious students hurrying to final exams. Once, long ago, I'd done that. It had been important then and so I silently wished them well. They were a colorful lot, this year's crop, maybe hoping that jobs would be attracted to their shared unisex bright shirts and faded jeans like moths to summer neons.

Inside the hospital I managed to talk my way past a suspicious receptionist and took the elevator up to the intensive care wing. Nurses ignored me, but doctors I passed in the outer corridor examined me for symptoms. I, in turn, ignored the doctors. I'd had my morning five-mile run and felt I was safe, at least for this day.

Steinmetz lay in a white bed with wires attached to his chest and a tube in his nose. There was a small window between his room and the hall—perhaps so a patient could look out at his possible survivors—and I

thought he saw me as I came down the corridor, but I
wasn't certain. Then a white-clad nurse inside the room
pulled a curtain over the window.

My friend Doc Buckner stood by the door. He
stopped me with an imperative gesture.

"I'd not have asked you to come here, but he's been so
damned agitated I thought he'd be better off seeing you
than not seeing you. The emergency ambulance techs
said he'd been at his mailbox and then had a stroke between the box and his door. He fell over and dropped
his mail and a neighbor saw the incident and called.
The techs thought he was gone when they brought him,
but we got him back easily enough and now he's conscious and moving and that's a good sign. If he'd gotten
inside his house and then had the stroke he could easily
have died before anyone found him." He shook his
head, irritated at both me and death, equating us, and
perhaps finding me the more wanting. We live for a
time and then we die, but doctors, good doctors, are
difficult to force that truth upon. The best of them believe they can cure all. They view each patient-death as
a personal insult. Buckner was that kind of doctor.

"How's he doing now?"

Buckner leaned close. "By all rights he ought to be
sprouting wings, Robak. The blood vessels in his head
can't be much stronger than toilet paper. This is the
fourth time we've had him here in the last three years,
two heart attacks, two strokes." He raised his eyebrows.
"He ought to be dead, but he's one tough old bourbon
bastard. I want you to go in and see what he wants so
bad, what's got him so riled up. He won't or can't tell
me. I know it's something he found in his mailbox. He's
got one piece of that mail clutched in his good hand. He
won't let us take it. He said your name a couple of

times. Then he stopped talking. I called the sheriff's office and you'd just gone from there, but then a police
car found you. Now you go in and come back out as
quick as you can. Maybe he'll survive again with rest
and medicine and luck. Right now he needs sleep, not
questions." He gave me a tiny smile to show he didn't
mean what was coming. "Sleep would benefit more
than anything except my miracle medical care."

I nodded solemnly. "Sure, Doc, you're the doctor."
I'd known Doc Buckner for a long time, long enough
for him to put up with an occasional bad line. "Okay to
go inside now?"

"Quickstep," he warned again. "Then I don't want
you or anyone else around him for a time. The only
thing he'll see is a full-time crew of special duty nurses.
And, if he makes it and begins to improve, I don't want
you or Jake sneaking him in any whiskey. That'll be the
first rule he tries to evade. And you'll be the first persons he conspires with."

I moved past Buckner and sniffed the room's inner air
gingerly. The intensive care area smelled pungently of
strong drugs, non-drinkable alcohol, and those who'd
not made it, a smell of the dead and living, of dying and
fighting to live intermixed. It seemed no place for a man
like Judge Steinmetz, *of counsel* to my law firm, a man
fond of chewing unlighted cigars and drinking Early
Times and water in tall glasses. A year before I'd heard
that Doc Buckner had put him on a one drink a day
diet. It hadn't much affected Steinmetz. He'd bought a
bigger glass. He was, he told me sullenly under my
questioning then, too old to take orders from anyone
but God.

I walked close to Steinmetz's bed. The room was dim.
A pretty nurse watched me alertly from a corner, per-

haps fearing evil. Steinmetz weakly inspected me. Someone had removed his false teeth and he appeared slightly out of focus because of the vacancy. His eyes seemed faded and his color was greyish. He clutched something in his right hand and managed to lift that hand a fraction from the pillow. I gently took what he offered. It was a piece of paper from a lined yellow tablet. I opened the paper.

Someone had crudely printed words on the paper. I turned to the door light and read them: "Your daughter Gail Marie is sick. We need your money to help her or she could die. Give us fifty thousand dollars. Please. We have nothing. Wait for another message." Down below there was a printed signature. It read: "The 96'ers."

Steinmetz managed a tiny movement of his old, bald head. His eyes met mine again and I tried to read them. He fought to find words, but could not.

"You want me to look for her?" I asked.

A tiny nod. *Yes.*

"And the money?"

A more spirited downshake. *No.*

I wondered what he was thinking. He was a solitary man, apparently at peace within his self-erected solitude. He had his retirement checks from the bench and the money we paid him. Because he worked part-time in the office our pay was seldom much. To my knowledge that was all there was, but I'd never been observant about money, who had it, and who didn't. Steinmetz's wife was dead and his only child, Gail Marie, had vanished into the jackdaw streets and drug culture of sprawling Capitol City years back. He never spoke of her these days.

When he'd come to work for us I'd thought it was because he needed the money, but he'd refused most of the cases I sent him. He'd puttered where he wanted and ignored the rest.

"I'll look, Judge," I said. Maybe Gail Marie was his immortality. We all seek it.

He watched me for a long moment and then closed his eyes. In another minute he was sleeping. Buckner nodded approvingly at me from the door.

It took me three hours, after Jo's semiblessing, to get on my way north.

"I'll call tonight to tell you what's happening and to get updated on Steinmetz," I promised. "Check on him with the hospital or with Doc Buckner's office. It'll take time to find out how much this is going to affect him. Doc thought if he had another one he'd most likely die."

"Would that stop you searching for the daughter?"

"I don't know. I guess not. I'd need to tell her about Steinmetz and that he was dead."

Jo nodded and walked to the picture window and looked out it and I followed her gaze. Outside our son Joe played in a swing set I'd erected for him a month back. The sun was warm and it was May again, his fifth May. I remembered I'd promised to take both of them to see the Cincinnati Reds at Riverfront soon, but now that must wait for a while.

"Why you and not the police?"

"I guess because he's my friend. But I won't try looking without police help. I'm not stupid and I know some police up there. Remember I did a term once in the state legislature?"

"I remember, even if that time was before I knew you. You told me about it and you also said that Capitol City was one of the worst places on earth."

"That was years ago. I don't know how it is now." I

thought on it. "Probably changed." *Change comes hard, but it's easy to say that change has happened.*

Her kiss at the door was cool and perfunctory and she kept her eyes on Joe in the yard and away from me.

"Hurry home," she said, perhaps not that certain about it.

Before heading for the interstate I did several other things. First I went past Steinmetz's house. Someone, possibly one of the ambulance people, had used Steinmetz's key and put the rest of his spilled mail in a neat stack inside the door on a table. I found it there after I opened the door with my key, one that Steinmetz had given me a year back when he'd needed me to fetch things while he was in the hospital on an earlier admission.

I found a lone, opened envelope among the bills and assorted mail. It was a cheap, white long one, and looked like the kind you could buy in dime stores and supermarkets. It bore no return address and no postmark. I guessed that it had held the note I'd read in Steinmetz's hospital room. I picked up the envelope carefully by inserting an unopened ballpoint pen inside it.

I looked through Steinmetz's small house. There seemed to be little else of interest, but in an old album by the fireplace I found some photos. Some were of Steinmetz and his wife and the girl. As she'd grown older a few were of the girl alone. Gail Marie Steinmetz, then age eighteen or so. She had Steinmetz's stubborn look intermingled with some of her mother's beauty. She was well, if somewhat sturdily, built.

I remembered her from years back. She'd been coltish in appearance when I'd first met her, but dead serious and intent on the world around her. In Bington, then and now, that had included the drugs of her peers. Some of the young experiment and retreat after being mildly burned, some wisely resist, and a few become devotees. Gail had been one of those who had taken the hook and then had become too stubborn or captured to give it up.

I used Steinmetz's phone to call the office and tell them where I was going and that I'd be back in a few days. No one cared enough to protest a lot there.

I took photo and envelope with me to the Bington police station. There I called on George Gentrup. He was the Bington police chief and we were friends of a sort. He was far better friends with Steinmetz than with me.

"How does he figure you can help him?" he asked, deadpan. "Why, for instance, would he ask you to look instead of me?"

"Maybe because I know his daughter. I knew her well enough when she was here to probably recognize her if I saw her again. I doubt you would or could. Steinmetz knows that. She had a kind of 'thing' for me when she was seventeen or so, a crush. Lord knows why."

"True," he said. "You might have been pretty then, but my, my, look at you now. And you want me to see if I can lift any fingerprints off the note Steinmetz showed you at the hospital and/or this envelope?"

"Yes." I explained the care I'd used in transporting the envelope while he listened.

"It doesn't have a stamp or postmark," he said, looking down at it.

"That's because it was hand delivered to his mailbox. Us real detectives saw that quick."

"That means whoever hand delivered it was here in Bington."

"Congratulations."

"And chances are the deliverer probably knows more about fingerprints than you or me. But I can try, Robak." He gave me a curious look. "And while I'm trying that just exactly what will you be doing?"

"I'll be driving up to Capitol City. I used to know some people up there. Maybe I can find her or find out what's happened to her. That's where she went when she ran away. Maybe she's still there. The note says she's sick. Someone wrote it. What someone? Who wants Steinmetz's fifty thousand dollars, if he's got it? Who sent him the note that probably caused his stroke?"

Gentrup grimaced like a baby with a gas pain. "Who-who is right. I think I remember the girl vaguely. A hardhead. Some juvenile pick-ups on her record. Drinking and drugs. Why'd she leave home?"

"I'd guess it was a difference in philosophies. She was a fairly typical college girl when I knew her, but Steinmetz said she was aloof and independent from her fifteenth birthday on. She fell out with her mother over drugs and the Vietnam War and maybe anything else they could find to bicker about. When Steinmetz took his wife's side the girl just packed her things one day and moved on. A nineteen-year-old in a snit and with a warm desire for booze, Mary Jane and maybe some other, meaner drugs. Once, when Steinmetz and I were drinking and he got unnaturally talkative, he said they'd hoped she'd come quickly back. But soon it was six months, then a year. Now it's been fifteen years or more. A long snit."

"It happens. Letters?"

"No. Nothing from her until this, if it really has to do with her. Someone may know about her and be trying to run a scam." I examined him. "Maybe you could watch the mailbox for anything else that might come, like maybe a more definite ransom note, if that's what the first note is intended to be."

"Sure. I'll check the mail. Plus I'll notify the right people. The F.B.I., the state police, and the police in Capitol City. I suppose it could be a kidnapping if she's not in on it herself. It's extortion at the least, but it's bland and would be tough to get a conviction on with just this letter. Did the daughter come back for the funeral when her mother died?"

"No. Steinmetz did his best to find her then, but couldn't in the time available. After the funeral he lost interest in running her down. From what I know he hasn't seen her since the day she walked away. I don't know if he wants to see her now. All I got from him was that he wants me to find her and find out about the note."

"He has more faith in your abilities than I do," Gentrup said, smiling a little. "Once the feds see the note they could get interested. If they do, then you could be in the way."

"Steinmetz also has more faith in me than I do," I admitted. "But I promised him and it eased him, so I'll go up to Capitol City and look some and try to stay from underfoot if anything official gets going. If he gets better then you get in to see him and tell him I'm looking around, but that I might be a problem because there are others looking. I imagine he'll want me to quit then and I'll do it happily." I thought of something. "When you check his house, try to figure out whether anyone's been inside. It's possible that whoever left the note saw him pass out and sneaked in for a peek before all of the excitement."

He nodded agreeably, liking my words about getting out of the way. "I know a guy up in Capitol City Police who's pretty good. Name's Lemon, Arthur Lemon. He's a detective and he's better than competent. Go see him. I'll call him and tell him you'll stop by. So you *will* stop by." The last was an order.

"Thanks, George."

He sniffed. "Sending you up there is like sending a five-year-old to officiate at a gang rumble."

I nodded humbly in agreement. George had little faith in me, but it might be more than I had. I thought of one more thing.

"If you want pictures of the daughter, there are some others in the album by Steinmetz's fireplace. And he's had the same cleaning lady for years. A Mrs. Milton who lives over the river. Someone might check her to see if she knows anything." I dug out my key to Steinmetz's house and surrendered it to him.

He took it and then issued me a few more instructions about not messing up things, and I promised to abide faithfully by his ideas concerning the red-eyed law and my conduct-to-be in Capitol City, not even crossing my fingers as I bowed and scraped.

I took the interstate north and left sweet Bington and the river behind. The trees were green along the interstate and someone had redone the white lines at the outer edges of the lanes. Ah, highway workers and spring combined. It was enough to renew one's faith in the political system. I noticed that other drivers had their windows down and so I lowered mine and got my dose of fresh air mixed with the area carcinogens. Monkey see and do. The temperature was about seventy.

It was Wednesday, a Jug Finder golfing day, and I wondered how they'd do without me to keep score. Probably better.

In two hours I was in downtown Capitol City. I was familiar with the city. I'd done two legislative sessions there, one a year for my two-year term. I'd been there afterward for various legal seminars, conventions, and meetings. It wasn't my favorite city. I vaguely like Louisville, Memphis, Saint Louis, New Orleans, San Francisco, Indianapolis, and some others, but Capitol City has always reminded me of an aging whore masquerading as a gospel singer. It's a town of paint and powder, new buildings, and skywalks between old buildings. It tends, like many cities, to be unsafe at night and unremarkable by day. About two million people laughingly call Capitol City and its suburbs home, perhaps because they've been ordered out of other places and have nowhere else to roost. I didn't hate Capitol City. I just knew it.

The Blue Hotel, where once I'd stayed as a legislator, had been torn down and made into an overpriced tenstory parking lot. To replace it I found a semirespectable-appearing motel close to the downtown area. It was part of a national chain. That reassured me and so I parked there and entered. For many a dollar a whitetoothed, unctuous clerk found me a room and gave me a printed map showing me how to get to it. He made a copy of my credit card and then released me. I went back outside and looked around. Across the street there was a Wendy's and on a far corner, across from the Shell station, a Burger King, so I'd not starve. There'd been a bar in the lobby and on a far corner there were two more. I'd not die of thirst either.

A good section of town. Yes sir. My kind of section.

I found my room and settled my stuff in. I left the car behind and started toward downtown. I crossed the street and walked past one of the bars. The front door was propped open and loud music sounded. I stuck my head inside the door.

Two go-go girls, who had both reached the age where they could better be described as gone-gone girls, gyrated alarmingly at opposite ends of a long, uncrowded bar, probably causing their blood pressure to elevate and their diabetes to activate. Their upper clothing was nonexistent, their lower minimal. Maybe, I thought, the dance was done to cool off in the heat.

A fat bartender beckoned. "Join the fun."

"Later," I called heartily. "Next century, if I live that long," I said to myself as I moved on.

The streets were crowded downtown. The male pedestrians mostly ignored each other and me. If you were noticed in Capitol City it was usually a surly notice, full of hate, fear, or contempt. The females either ignored you or estimated your wealth by your clothes.

Each year the denizens of the cities get bolder and meaner, more savage, and angrier. They deal their drugs openly, they mug each other in broad daylight, they rob and kill without fear of the overworked police, who are hampered by laws that are unresponsive to the problems. Trials are long and expensive, appeals longer and more expensive. I thought that one day soon, here or in New York or Chicago or L.A., a time would come when the pushers, pimps, and perverts would go for each other's vital spots when they passed on the street, firing guns, slashing with knives, scissors, and hatpins. Then the survivors would hunt the other survivors for food when the shelves emptied at the nearest twenty-four-hour convenience store.

But not quite yet. For now they were satisfied with occasional riots, graffiti, and television violence.

I knew where the Municipal Building was. I found it and inquired inside for a police detective named Arthur Lemon.

A bored desk lady in uniform inquired about my business with him. She looked mean and had buck teeth so I truthfully told her. Her face remained bored. Maybe it was her professional look.

"You sit and wait over there," she said, pointing me to folding seats, all empty now. "Don't you bother nothin'. Just sit quiet in the seat where I'm telling you to sit. Don't drink nothin' or eat nothin'. I'll try to see if I can find him."

I nodded obediently and she left me.

After a long while a small man came out a side door and into the waiting room. He was smoking a cigarette and he was late fortyish, which is an age I've known well. His hair was gone on top and I thought he might have recolored the sides. They were falsely jet black, maybe in an attempt to fool both himself and the world that he was younger.

"You Robak?"

"Yes sir."

"I'm Lemon. Follow me on back."

I followed. Inside the headquarters there was activity. Men and women typed, asked questions on the telephone, but mostly they drank coffee. We passed a holding cell where a dry-eyed old man sat staring at the floor, muttering highly inventive curse word phrases to himself. I hesitated momentarily, picking up a new phrase or two, but then I followed along again.

Lemon led me to a tiny office with a desk and two chairs. He took the chair behind the desk.

"Sit there. I got a call from George Gentrup. He told me you were looking for a girl who's been missing and read me a note wanting money for her. He also said he'd called the F.B.I. and they aren't much interested yet." His lip curled and I nodded agreeably, knowing that most police don't like the federals. "They need something more, I guess, like maybe one of her ears or fingers. Gentrup told me to tell you he also checked inside a house and couldn't be certain whether anyone had been in it or not. He wants you to take a look with him when you go back to Bington."

I nodded. "How do you know George?"

He shrugged amiably. "From here and there. I get down to Bington for football games at the university and sometimes I like to fish. George is a fisherman. He knows some lakes and ponds and he also likes football. Kindred spirits." He smiled and it changed his face, turning it from something foxy to something genuine. "I went to school down there years ago. Got my degree just like I was human or something."

"Me also."

"That makes us both alums," he said and then his face changed back again to his business face. "So how do you want me to help?"

"You ever heard of any group around the city called the '96'ers'?"

"Not that I recall. George gave me that name on the note and so I ran it through the computer and came up dry. I asked narcotics, but it didn't mean anything to them either. But out on 96th Street there are some tough areas and your missing lady could be a resident out there. My guess is that this ex-judge's daughter, or her pals, are maybe running a con game to raise some quick drug bucks. The resident F.B.I. guy and I talked and that's how they're viewing it for now. And I think your George Gentrup has the same notion."

"How about Gail Marie Steinmetz personally? Do you have any record on her, wants or warrants?"

"Nothing under that name."

"Maybe she changed it by marriage or choice. Remember when she came here she was running away from troubles in Bington."

"She could have changed it for sure." He opened his desk and pulled out a phone book. "There are some Steinmetzes in here, but she ain't one of them. I had someone call and no local person named Steinmetz would even admit knowing her."

"Thanks for trying."

"*De nada.*"

"Are you Spanish?" I asked without smiling.

"Nope," he answered, grinning. "George said you were unusually insolent."

"Just another alum. Where do the druggies in your city mainly congregate?"

"All over. You can buy pot from half the local bartenders, cocaine from maybe a thousand small-time dealers. Now and again we bust one or two. A few times we've gotten the bustee to tell us his upward connection, but they've seldom proved out and some who've opened their mouths have got shot, or jumped out high windows, got hit by cars, or strongly overdosed." He shook his head. "We patrol the streets, we guard the suburbs, we do traffic, and the best we can with the rest of the job. Last year the city fathers cut our budget nine percent. That tells you how necessary they think we are. I have three years, six months, five days, and maybe about fifteen hours to go before retirement, but who's counting?" He stopped for a moment and looked me over. "You know where a lot of our drugs come from these days?"

"No."

"They come in from the Ohio River and on up the interstate to my fair city from your lovely university town of Bington."

"I hadn't heard that."

"Well they do. Sometimes George will make a big bust down your way and some of my locals will be involved in it, having passed on information. Sometimes we'll catch one of your transporters up here. But running the stuff up the river in bulk is a lot safer than trying to transport it up the interstates these days. George will tell you. You know how both of us got onto it?"

"No, and I'm interested."

"You can buy pot and cocaine cheaper in Bington than you can here in the city. Ain't that a gas?"

I waited to see if there was more, but he dug through some papers on his desk and gave me an impatient look.

I got up obligingly. "Okay. Thankee kindly for the help. I'll stick around a while and take me a look. Maybe out on 96th Street."

"Whatever," he answered, affable now that I was leaving. "Just don't you violate our ordinances by overparking or anything bad like that." He smiled at me and I found myself liking him a little. "You find something, you call me. And maybe there'll soon be another letter that'll interest the federal boys." He examined me and seemed unimpressed. "Where you staying?"

I told him.

"If you want to buy yourself a little recreational pot try any of the bars in the area of your motel. And keep one hand on your billfold and the other on your crotch."

"That sounds like good advice."

"Ta ta." He went back to his papers.

THREE

"Steinmetz's Memoirs" (manuscript) page 127: "The oddest thing about this law business is that sometimes, just to throw you out of kilter and off stride, someone will tell you the plain, unvarnished truth."

BACK AT THE MOTEL I dug out from the glove compartment a rumpled city map I'd acquired during a long-ago legislative session and found 96th Street where I knew it had to be, miles north of downtown, running east and west. Maybe the 96'ers' signature did mean 96th Street. I've never found that people who want to con you or steal from you are automatically smart or devious.

I drove out that way, dodging in and out of downtown traffic for a time, but then having it thin for the laboring LTD and me when I got north.

I found 96th and drove it from one end to the other, a long drive. Mostly it was small houses, some of them boarded up, and ramshackle apartment buildings. Some vacant areas marked by "for sale" signs. Cities grow haphazardly and 96th was one of those throwaway areas left over as the city moved on in other directions.

There were some business areas where the main thoroughfares running north and south crossed it. Where Emmetson Boulevard crossed 96th there was a large concentration of bars, clubs, gasoline stations, chain supermarkets, and porno book and movie shops. It seemed worth checking out, but I decided the dark hours would be a better time. Now, in the warm late afternoon, the business area, as I cruised it, was just coming to life.

Two young men, holding hands, crossed in front of me at a red light. They smiled for each other, oblivious of the world around them. *Ah, young love.*

A handsome woman with a painted, professional look crossed behind them, saw me in my car and gave me a smile, not even noticing the two men in front of her. On a far corner a man with an open bottle of wine held desperately to a telephone pole. Business at a nearby porno shop seemed brisk.

I saw no police cars.

I tried to remember if Gail had had boyfriends in the time I'd known her or known about her. I couldn't remember any, but that didn't mean she'd not had them. I'd not known her that well.

I got the LTD filled with gas at a neighborhood discount gas station which advertised it took all credit cards. I did the job myself, operating the hose manually and carefully. Some gas stations these days have shutoffs that don't work well. *A penny here, a penny there.*

When I completed the job, the aging attendant took my Shell plastic card grudgingly, ran it through a charging machine by the pumps, and verified the license tag number I supplied by going to the back of my car and looking at it. He was a short, balding man. He watched the street in front of him with care and me with some suspicion after seeing my license plate wasn't local.

"Looks like a neighborhood where things could be tough," I said.

He frowned. "Tough is right. Some of them damn

freaks out there, male, female, or mixed, would kill you for a quarter. The place here may be the only station in town that closes come dusk. Ain't safe after dark. Used to be open all night, but we got robbed lots. A year back I got shot up. Bastard just pulled up, run his window down, and when I came running, did target practice on me. Took money, oil, cigarettes, and candy, and even a couple of tires. I got his license number while I was on the concrete not moving." He shook his head. "Didn't do a damn bit of good. Stolen car. But I'll know his grinning face if I see it again. I'm lucky to be alive. So the owners started closing her down at dusk. The way business is, my bet is they'll close the whole shooting match sometime soon. Maybe sell it to another of them places for pretty perverts."

"Suppose someone was looking to find someone around here? Someone who had disappeared?"

"Male or female?" he asked, without much interest other than to gossip. "Lots of the he's around here are into heing for fun and some of the she's are into sheing for their good times."

"This friend's female. She left her parents because she got into drugs. I don't know for sure about her sex life."

He nodded doubtfully. "Well you could check around, but you probably won't find out a lot. Most folks out here won't answer questions 'cause they don't believe they ought to, but maybe you can find someone who will. If you're looking for someone to talk with I'd say the place to start would be Jack's Bar. Around the corner and up about a block. You'll get treated polite if you act polite. It's mostly black, but it ain't the kind of place where they get mean when whites come inside. If you go there I'll ask you not tell who directed you to it.

I have a drink there now and again myself and I don't want no more trouble than I've already got."

"Why do you drink there?" I asked curiously. "I mean with you getting shot a block away?"

"Getting shot made me well known," he said, grinning. "They pour a decent drink at Jack's, and trouble starts, then they look out for regular customers. And it's an orderly kind of place." He shook his head and looked out again at the street. "Got to go someplace or go crazy. For fun, I mean. Can't live your life under lock and key. Told my wife that, but she decided to leave me anyhow."

"I guess you're right about going someplace. Thanks for the information." I gave him five dollars and left him smiling at my back bumper. *The world wasn't all bad when someone gave you money.*

I took one more trip through the immediate neighborhood. A billboard which advertised Camels had dirty words sprayed on it and the cigarette looked like something out of a porno movie. One man sold another man two foil packets as I waited at a stoplight. A white man and a black woman cursed at each other drunkenly at the next.

I drove back to my motel and parked in the lot. I got out and looked around inside. There was a high fence with a triangle of barbed wire at the top around the motel. There was an opening in front, but, after dark, the desk was set up to observe who entered and exited.

A man came out of a little guardhouse near the motel building. He had a list in hand and I saw him glance at my license plate and then, satisfied, return to his cement block home.

I shivered involuntarily. *One day soon we'll all live in*

enclaves, afraid of those who live inside with us, more afraid of those who live outside our fences. Then it will slowly or quickly get worse.

In spite of or because of the guard I locked the LTD and walked back to the main entrance of the motel. The lobby was quiet. I entered the motel bar and sat on a plush stool. At the far end of the bar a thin, lightly bearded bartender argued loud baseball with one lone customer. He saw me and gave a sour wait-one-moment look.

I waited. There was a bowl of nuts nearby. I scooped a few out and chewed them. They were stale.

In a while the bartender decided I'd paid enough penance for disturbing him and approached me. I ordered Canadian and water. I put a ten dollar bill on the bar. I'm never sure, in cities, what the cost will be. He took the bill when he brought my drink. He laid a five, two singles, and some change on the bar. I pushed the five toward him and he took it quickly.

"Who do I have to kill?" he asked.

"You know where 96th Street meets Emmetson?"

"I know it. It's too lively out that way for me. Some of the bars are gay, some aren't. You can get yourself stomped you say or do the wrong thing in the wrong bar, male or female."

I sipped the Canadian. I doubted it was the brand I'd ordered, but it was tolerable. "If I wanted to buy a little something, just enough for me and a friend for a day or two, could I get it out there?"

"You can get drugs anyplace around the city," he said without a smile. "That's if you look okay and check out okay." He shook his head and examined me some more. "I could be wrong and I ain't picking at you, but you don't look to me like someone buying for the fun of the purchase. And I don't think you're into selling either."

"Thank you for your candor," I said.

He shrugged and went back down the bar to his baseball companion. Both of them watched me and the discussion became quieter. I finished my drink and left the rest of the ten on the counter when I exited. The bartender gave me a wave before he rushed for the money.

Across the street from the motel, as it grew dark, I dined on a Wendy's cheeseburger with tomato, lettuce, and mayo, gourmet style. Two tired, young ladies entered as I exited. One of them brushed past me closely and I held onto my billfold.

"Want some fun?" she asked.

"Not just now, but I do hate missing it," I said and watched her pout.

I crossed the street again and went up to my room. I'd left my bag on the bed and no one had bothered it when I checked the hair I'd laid across the lock.

I called Jo and told her where I was. She told me she'd checked the hospital and that Steinmetz was still listed as critical, but stable. George Gentrup had not called. I told Jo that I hoped to come back tomorrow, but not to count on it.

I waited an hour plus, watching a television screen full of sitcoms, listening to their collection of silly, canned, and usually inappropriate laughter. Then I got the LTD and drove north again. The traffic, now that the evening rush hour was over, was light.

Jack's Bar was medium dark inside. The walls were decorated with old newspapers from around the time of World War I to present date. Headlines screamed about the Lindbergh baby, Martin Luther King, Da Nang,

and the PLO. Planes crashed, and earthquakes happened. Mostly people killed other people, our most popular national pastime. The newspapers made an effec-
tive wall covering.

I took a vacant seat at the bar. The place was crowded
and I smelled the faint sweet smell of pot, not strong,
but obvious.

A black, smiling bartender brought me the kind of
Canadian I'd ordered and took a bit more money than
I'd paid at the motel bar. I sat thinking, trying to figure
what might be my next move. If I couldn't convince the
motel bartender that I was into drugs, I doubted I'd
convince anyone in this place.

So I sat.

A tall, strong-looking black man took the bar seat
next to me and, in a while, a white, stunningly lovely
woman came for him. I thought I'd seen the black man
before and wondered where it had been. There was a
vacant bar seat next to mine so I moved over one. They
smiled thanks and then talked to each other in low
voices. I heard some of the words, but the sense of it was
beyond me. All I could pick up were names now and
then. I decided hers was Faye and his was Jack or Jock.
The rest was the new speech of the cities. Some of it's
black, but not all. Some comes from drugs, some from
pop music. A few things were singly recognizable because I'd heard the language before in Bington, Bington
being a university town and therefore heavily into
drugs and pop music. I've never understood it really
well, but I'm tolerant of it. I want to live with the world
around me, not run it or police it. The fact not everyone
feels that way keeps me, as a lawyer, in business.

I ordered another drink and debated with myself
while the smiling bartender brought it. As the bar-

tender walked away from me the black man seated near me stopped him with a wave. The bartender leaned close and listened. He nodded and came back to me.

"Jack says you a polite man and he's buying you this drink." He smiled more widely and I smiled also and nodded thanks. I turned to the man next to me. He sat alertly on his stool, watching me in the bar mirror, obviously curious.

"Thanks. I could also use some good advice. Could I maybe ask you some questions about this area?"

He shook his head, smiling. "All I'll promise is I'll listen to the questions," he said. "I don't remember seeing you in here before."

I thought about the pot fable plus other possible lies and then abandoned the ideas. "That's true. I'm a lawyer in Bington. I'm looking for someone who once was maybe in this neighborhood and might still be around here."

He shrugged, eyes unreadable. "Could I take a look inside your billfold before we talk more?" he asked in a deep voice.

I got it out and handed it to him. He found my driver's license and compared the picture on it to me. He went through my cards. Then he handed my billfold back to me.

"I guess you are what you say you are, but that doesn't buy you answers. Sometimes information costs lots around here, if it can be bought at all."

"There's not any big money available. If there was I'd have hired someone else to do the looking and not be trying it myself." I got out the picture and showed it to him. "This is a dozen years old. And it's the latest one we had. I'm trying to find the lady in the picture."

He took the photo and examined it. "Kind of a chunk," he said. "What's her name?"

"The name she got when she was born was Gail Marie Steinmetz. I doubt much if that lasted long up here."

He looked at the picture some more. He handed it to the girl next to him and then turned back to me. "Until you moved over a stool I thought maybe you was a new undercover cop, but then I see your suit's too good, you don't swill down your drinks, and you don't do a lot of heavy watching, and you ain't upset because my lady's white." He grinned.

"Not upset. Maybe envious."

The girl beside him whispered in his ear and he nodded.

"I don't know her, but Marta Faye thinks she might have seen her in the neighborhood. She's a lot thinner now. There are a bunch of women-only joints in the neighborhood. The biggest is a place called the Pleasure Palace. It's up the street. You can go in there and they'll serve you a drink at the bar, but they won't answer many of your questions. You can watch what goes on though and you'll be treated okay." He smiled some more. "The other big lezzie place is Mary O'Leans Shift, across the street. If I was you I'd not go in there. It's rough at times. There's some class ladies that go there, but some who use it are tough and don't like men being close by at all. Lesbians are like the rest of us. Some are good, some are bad. It's about the same percentage as you and me and the rest of the world. For a hundred, if you can come up with that much, I'll send Miss Marta Faye to inquire for you in both places. She's got friends there. You can wait here."

He knew there was more than that in my billfold so I got it out. "Deal."

"Your place?" I asked politely.

"A piece of it is mine now. I started coming here before I owned any of it because of the name being the same as mine. The Jack who originally owned it is a long time dead. Got himself shot in a card game. Why are you looking for this lady?"

"Her father's a friend. He's sick. Had a bad stroke. He and the daughter fell out years back. He wants to see her now. He used to be the circuit judge down in Mojeff County, Bington."

"I know the town some. I went to school down there."

I nodded and smiled. "The world is full of us alums," I said. "It's a big school."

"That's a fact. And that's the whole truth of it?" he asked, trying to read my face.

I thought he was trying to decide things in my favor and so I went further. "Most of it. Someone sent him a note wanting money for the missing daughter or for themselves. He knew she'd come here when she left so it seemed a good place to start."

He gave the lithe, lovely girl some of the money and she got up from the stool and vanished out the front door.

I looked at his empty glass and mine. "Can I repay the drink while I wait?"

He nodded. "Sure. I'm a J&B man, rocks."

I waved at the bartender and gave the order. We waited. Once a white man came past and talked in low, intense tones to Jack, ignoring me. Jack replied in a soft voice. When the white man had finished his business, other people, black and white, came past and Jack nodded or conversed or slapped them on the back. His eyes watched everywhere.

The bartender brought our drinks. He was sweating a bit from exertion and I saw the place had filled up more. I looked around again and saw that the wall nearest me seemed to be full of sports stories.

"Okay if I take a look at that wall?" I asked Jack.

"Sure. Help yourself. I'll save your seat."

I left my drink and went over to the wall. Maris slammed his sixty-first home run, A. J. Foyt won another 500. There was an autograph on that one. Pete Rose got his record hit and Indiana University won another basketball NCAA behind bad/good Bobby. Boxers rose, faded, fell, and wrote poor doggerel.

I saw Jack's picture three times. He'd played his football at State U. in Bington and, later, for the Lions. His full name and nickname was John Thaddeus "Father" Brown. I remembered seeing him block a field goal on a cold November afternoon years back. He'd been good.

I read on.

After a while Jack's girl came back. She took the seat on the far side of Jack and they whispered a bit. I went back to the bar and took the seat he'd saved for me. Jack turned to me.

"Maybe the lady you're looking for used to be around those lezzy places with a fat, black lady named Wanda. They say, both places, that no one's seen them for a few weeks. The two of them lived together, last known, at the 'Acres.' It's a rundown kind of apartment about a mile north on Emmetson, right side of the street. Wanda is Wanda Carson, your lady was going under the name of Marie Stone." He smiled. "That ought to be worth your hundred."

Steinmetz to Stone.

"Thank you both," I said. "It's more than worth it."

The girl gave me a beautiful smile. Jack Brown said amiably to me: "You sit nice and read nice. You don't bother anyone and you ain't loud or pushy. You make room. Lot of people they don't make room for anyone these days. Sometimes such causes trouble." He smiled down at the bar and took a long look around his room. He held his scotch in a huge hand and took a tiny nip. "But you watch close from now on. Everywhere. My lady says there was some interest in both places that there was a someone in town and looking, and to get what she found she had to tell your story. It'll get spread in the female-female sorority."

"That's okay. And thanks again." I examined him. "I thought you looked familiar when I first saw you. You look like you could still play football."

He grinned at the compliment. "Too old, fat, and brittle. And I'm in business." He tapped me on the arm gently. "You look in good shape. What do you weigh?"

"About one-ninety."

He smiled wisely. "I guessed less than that. You buy your clothes a little big and it makes you look thinner. Maybe you're good, but lots of them out there would likely eat you alive. So you watch your butt. If you can, you maybe come back up the line and tell us what happened."

"I'll do that," I said, liking him. "And I'll try to bring a football friend you'd like."

"Who's that."

"Sam King."

He nodded knowledgeably. "I've seen him play. He'd have been something if he'd not torn up his knee."

We shook hands and I nodded politely at his lady.

I left more money on the bar and went out into the

night. Outside a couple of panhandlers tried me, but I went quickly past them, reluctant to pull out any money, even change. I unlocked the LTD and drove north.

I'd been lucky. A gap of years had perhaps been narrowed to weeks. I felt very bright and smart and glad I'd not tried the pot-cocaine fantasy.

Honesty can be the best policy. I know that, but being a lawyer, I've tried other ways.

The Acres Apartments was a medium-sized, run-down brick, seven stories high, four apartments to each floor once I was inside and could see the mailboxes. There was no doorman and the front door yielded to my touch. There was an elevator, but it was keyed.

I found no Wanda Carson or Marie Stone on the line of mailboxes. I did see that there were boxes without names so there probably were empty apartments.

A Hans Daushke in Apartment 1A listed himself as the building superintendant and rental agent. I walked to his door and buzzed. In a while he came on through a speaker above his buzzer.

"Yeah?"

"I'm trying to find some people. My name's Robak and I'm a lawyer from down in Bington. The people I'm looking for would be a black lady, big woman. Then there's a smaller white girl. They were, I've been told, living together. There might be some others with them. The black girl was named Wanda Carson, the white one was Marie Stone. I don't have other names. I need to find Marie Stone or the others, if they can tell me where Marie Stone is."

"The one you really want is Marie Stone?"

"Yes. But if I can't find her I'd like to find one of the others."

"There was three of them lived here," he said, after a pause. "The lease was in Marie Stone's name. Then there were some others who hung around and might have stayed with them some. They all left three weeks ago. Left me hanging out with some rent due. Moved out in the middle of the night, quiet-like. I woke up and they was gone."

"What was the third girl's name?"

"I don't know. After they'd been here for a while she moved in with them. She never said diddly and I never got her name." He laughed unpleasantly. "I wasn't close with any of them, if you get what I mean."

"Any idea of where they might have gone when they left?"

"No. I went to their door next day to try again on the rent the black one had promised and found the place bare except for their garbage. Good riddance if they hadn't stuck me." He paused. "If you find them around your town I'd sure appreciate it, and my owners would appreciate it, if you'd let us know their address. We got a real mean lawyer works for us. I bet you'd know him if I could think of his name."

"You think they went to Bington?"

"I don't know. I thought maybe yes because you say you're from Bington and looking for them. Stone said something about Bington once when I was fixin' something in their apartment. Having the three of them around here was a love problem, but no more than lots of other love problems I got. They had all these lady friends and they hung onto each other, kissy-like, but boys with boys do the same and so do boys with gals. I mean with all them diseases going around you'd think that people would be more careful. The gal without a name was kind of silly-pretty, wild hair, lots of lipstick." He sounded slightly scandalized that three women and their friends had lived in one of his apartments. "I try to be tolerant, but them kind and them other male ones we get in herds make it hard." He sighed. "I got to admit though that the worst trouble we have is men with women. They fight more and yell more. Last year one lady took a pistol to her boyfriend. Shot him in a place where no one wants to get shot. Love is a bad joke."

"Did you find out who moved my people out?"

"The apartments are ninety percent furnished. You can haul your stuff out and me not notice. We make them put up a deposit up front and I got that, but I guess I'll need to do some repainting." He stopped, but the speaker didn't click off so I waited. "I think maybe the one you're looking for, Marie Stone, was kind of off her feed and maybe sick-like. Too many bad drugs or AIDS or something. Thin, spaced-out at times, and irritable as a dog tied on a short rope."

I related that back to the note Steinmetz had gotten in his mailbox. Maybe Gail Marie was sick.

I was tired. It was time to go back to the motel and call it a night.

I wondered what I'd do and what Steinmetz would do if Gail Marie had AIDS.

"Thank you," I said. "If I locate them I'll send you a card with their addresses," I lied. "I've got your address."

FOUR

"Steinmetz's Memoirs" (manuscript) page 154: "I have been told that the only difference in cities and towns is in the number of people, but I keep praying it isn't so."

IN THE MORNING I'm an early riser. I'd run my usual route the morning before in Bington, so there was no inner compulsion inside me to run again on this day. The habit was strong, but it was an every other day kind of habit and, sometimes, not even that anymore. Besides, running in the city might get me mugged and result in the loss of my second-best pair of running shorts, which I'd brought in case I stayed long.

It had been cool enough the night before that I'd raised a reluctant window for fresh air. Now, in the early morning, I could smell the packing plants to the south, the exhaust from the busses, trucks, and cars on the streets, and the smell of too many people compressed into too small an area.

I shaved, brushed, and showered and looked over the mediocre results in the flawed motel mirror. There I was, Don Robak, pushing fifty, thinner some places than I'd been at thirty. The running hadn't removed the pot. It was still there, but it was an odd, small pot and I was used to it and so was Jo. It was a pot we sometimes discussed with minor hilarity, at least on Jo's part. It

looked like a small, hard hump on an emaciated camel.
A man who ran a health club in Bington had told me
how I could get rid of it and had tried to sell me a trial
membership in what looked to be a weightlifters group.
I'd declined. The running kept me thin and wiry and I
had no intention of trying to build large other lumps on
me by lifting weights.

I remembered, during the mirror inspection, that my
mother had thought I was something. *That had been nice
of her, but she'd been wrong.*

I dressed and hid the pot easily enough in a Hart
Schaffner & Marx executive-cut suit. I then breakfasted
on juice, an unbuttered English muffin, and black coffee
in a bustling downtown restaurant which only charged
me ten times what the meal was worth. The lady behind the cash register told me to "have a good day" and
I decided not to inform her I had other plans.

By ninish I was back in the Capitol City municipal
building and had talked my way past the bucktoothed
uniformed lady at the desk, who'd grown accustomed to
my face as I'd grown accustomed to hers. I sat in Detective Lemon's office, awaiting him. I could smell the odor
of boiling coffee, roach spray, and warming Xerox machines. Funny, all three smelled about the same.

Lemon came. He bore a steaming coffee and he
looked tired.

He viewed me sourly. "I got a lot to do today," he
complained to the world around him, which consisted
only of me. "You were in yesterday and a guy I know
called and said you'd be in, so I took some of my time
and did him a favor. But I don't know a thing more than
I did then."

"I do. She now goes by the name of Marie Stone. She
was hanging around the lesbian places, near Emmetson

and 96th. She lived, until a few weeks ago, at a place called The Acres, an apartment house up Emmetson at about 110th. She had something maybe going with another girl, this one a black lady named Wanda Carson. She may have had things going with some others. The super, named Hans Daushke, thought my girl was sick and also had an opinion it was possibly drugs or AIDS that had done the deed."

He looked at me for a long moment. His eyes were unreadable. He then inclined his head curtly. "Now I understand why George said to tell you what I could and let you fumble on your own. How'd you find out all that stuff?"

I decided it would be impolite telling him it hadn't been on the office computer.

"I got lucky asking questions."

"Sure," he said. Predictably he asked the question I was waiting for: "Want me to run the names through the computer?"

"That could help," I said.

"Get yourself coffee if you want," he offered expansively.

"No. I just had a big breakfast."

I sat in his office and waited after he was gone. The morning paper was on his desk and I thought about reading its fearsome stories of rape, robbery, and murder, but I'd not been invited to do that and so I didn't. His paper, his rapes, robberies, and murders. His city and not mine. Mine was Bington and I wanted to return there.

I daydreamed. In those idle dreams I saw Gail Marie as she'd been at age eighteen, a pretty girl with solemn eyes, slightly heavy, but not fat, and very intent on the life she saw. Her problem then had been that she'd in-

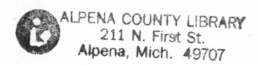

herited many of the things that had made her father a
first-class judge and a fine lawyer: stubbornness, an abil-
ity and a willingness to engage in argument, and no
desire to yield her found conclusions to the mores of the
world around her. In Steinmetz those matters were
attributes. In Gail Marie, growing up in the shiny drug-
laden world of her Bington peers, they'd been problems.

After a time Lemon returned. He had some printouts.
He took his chair.

"The black girl's been in for fighting and robbery and
crap like that a couple of times. Once the fight was in a
lesbian bar and she like to cleaned the whole place out
and did a lot of damage. Assaulted a plainclothes officer
when the officer tried to put a lid on the fight and broke
the officer's nose. No one prosecuted, I don't know why.
Maybe someone laughed the female officer out of prose-
cuting or maybe she was afraid someone would want to
know why she was in a lezzie bar. The black girl also
got picked up once for shoplifting and another time for
bigger stuff, armed robbery. She drew thirty days on
the shoplifting, reduced to conversion, and the armed
robbery got plea-bargained down to simple theft. She
got two years on that and was work-released in six
months. The last thing we got on her record is two
years back. Since then, nothing. Tough cookie, I'd
guess. And that area where they lived is tough also. We
made ourselves a drug bust in that apartment house
three months back. The word is we could make six
more in a two-block radius and still leave the area
dirty."

"No drug charges on Wanda Carson?"

"None of record."

"And Gail Marie?"

"Two minor drug arrests, both for marijuana less than thirty grams, misdemeanor stuff. She's got a driver's license under the name Marie Stone. It ran out last winter and hasn't been renewed yet." He shrugged it off as meaningless. "Lots of people don't renew until they get caught. She lived with a guy one time. Over the road trucker named Peter Yankosky who got killed in North Dakota in an accident. We show we notified her when he died. My guess is she then maybe drifted into one of the lesbian bars and found easy drugs and friendly companions. Lots of people, male and female, go both ways sexually." He smiled. "Or so the big boys at the poolroom tell me."

"Anything else?"

"I called your Hans Daushke at the apartments. You got most of it, but I got a car description. A '67 orange VW Beetle. Current plate number 100Z 34715, sold to Marie Stone. Find the car and maybe you'll find your lady."

I waited, knowing there was more.

"He said your girl was peculiar, acted like she didn't know what was going on, very dreamy. A few times she came down in the side yard to sunbathe not wearing any top. Spaced-out like. He didn't think, when I pinned him down, that she was sick with like AIDS or anything, just lost on drugs. I gave the VW license number and description to the dispatcher. He put it out. If anyone spots the car the report will eventually route on through to my desk."

"Does that mean a police officer would stop the car?"

He shook his head. "If the car's spotted then I'll get a report on it. Maybe late, maybe soon. No reason to stop the car—yet. Do you agree or do you want me to stop it?"

"I guess not. Not yet, anyway. And thank you. If someone does have Gail Marie I don't want to alarm them if I can avoid it." I got up. "Could I have the VW's tag number?"

He wrote it on a note card and I took the card and put it in my pocket. Lemon examined me once more looking for flaws in what I'd said and in my logic. Then he shook his head. "What now?"

"Bington," I said. "I'll call George Gentrup when I get back down there. He can take most of it from now on. I'll tell him to contact you if he finds anything new. One thing I'd like you to check if you can. Contact the authorities in North Dakota and make sure that Peter Yankosky's death was accidental."

"Okay, I'll do it and contact George for you if there was anything out of the way in it. If not I'll just not call him. Saves time that way."

I thought for a minute. "The letter in Steinmetz's mailbox wasn't placed there by a postman. Whoever put it in the box is either here or, more probably, in Bington." I nodded, thinking some more on that. *Maybe in Bington, watching and waiting.* "And I thank you again for your many courtesies."

He got up. There was a touch of the comic in him. He touched an imaginary cap bill. "Thank you also, Detective O'Robak."

I returned to my motel and checked out. In the parking lot, despite the high fence and security guards, someone had jerked off my radio antenna. Or maybe it had happened last night on 96th Street and I'd not noticed it until now. Ah well.

I drove out of Capitol City and took the interstate back home, happy to leave behind the smells and hurries of the large city. I can stand cities only in small bites. A single night in Capitol City was enough to last me for a long while.

I tried thinking about Steinmetz and his errant daughter and the rest of it as I drove, but not much came of it. A tiny something tugged at the back of my memory, vague as a night wind. There seemed to be something I was missing in my jigsaw. I tried but couldn't pinpoint it. *No matter.*

What I was missing came to me a moment later. Maybe there was a someone in Bington, a friend, or a friend of one of the other ladies. And maybe someone in Bington had heard from Gail Marie in the years she'd been gone. I could check.

The sun was out and the day was even fairer and finer than it had been the day before. It was good to be alive with lots of the golfing season left.

I decided that I didn't care that much about the antenna. The radio in the LTD hadn't worked for a long time anyway. Nothing much worked in the LTD.

I parked near the Bington police station. An officer I knew inside let me use the phone and I called Jo at work.

"You're back," she said, surprised and perhaps pleased.

"I called so you can make sure all the men get out of the house."

She laughed lightly. She was a happy person and laughed most times when I said stupid things like that, even if she didn't like for me to say them. She was a lady, and I was sometimes, perhaps many times, not a gentleman.

"I'll see you fivish at the country club," she said.

"Sure," I said. I'd momentarily forgotten that today was our Lovers League golf day. Wednesdays I played with the Jug Finders, Fridays she played in Ladies League. Then, in between on Thursdays, we played in the couples group. Lots of times we played on weekends. Her aunt babysat with Joe and loved it. *Ah, golf. And on the seventh day . . .*

George Gentrup appeared as I was rehanging the phone. He gave the desk officer an accusing look.

"Did you get his quarter for the call?"

I smiled appreciatively at his humor and followed him back to his office.

I told him what I'd learned. "It's very much drug country," I finished. "And Gail is into drugs and has a friend or a source who's supplying them to her. So maybe she's sick from that or something else and they've figured that Steinmetz can be their money supplier. For drugs, like you and Lemon think, or for whatever."

"All right," he said, digesting it. "There've been no other notes yet. About the only thing that's happened is that we tried to contact Mrs. Milton, who cleaned house for Steinmetz. She doesn't have a phone and the state boys across the river report they can't raise anyone at her house. Do you think you could go down to Steinmetz's with me and see if you think anything's gone? I need you to do that."

"I could try. The housekeeper would know more than me when you locate her."

"She may be visiting relatives or off on vacation. Until we find her I'm limited to you. Let's drive down there. You follow me. That way your clientele won't think you've just been arrested."

I smiled again at this new knee slapper. Gentrup never changed expression.

"How's Steinmetz doing?"

"The hospital says unchanged. I saw Doc Buckner when I was having a sumptuous breakfast at Hardee's and he thought he might be a little improved. Said he was somewhat more responsive than he'd been and there didn't seem to be any paralysis. But he still can't or won't try to talk and his movements are uncoordinated." He looked me over. "Buckner said if I saw you before he did that he'd like for you to contact him. He didn't say why." He frowned. "Everyone keeps secrets from me. Even Dutch Goldie the sheriff. He's got something going out in the county and he won't tell me what it is."

"I tell you all my secrets," I said, smiling.

"Only when they're worthless or you need help from me," he said acidly. "Let's go to Steinmetz's place. Then you can return to your office and create chaos and confusion there and at the courthouse instead of in my orderly, freshly cleaned, and well-administered police station."

"One thing Detective Lemon told me surprised me. He said a lot of Capitol City's drugs came through Bington, shipped up the river."

"True," George said shortly. "The river's wide and a lot less crowded than the public highways these days."

At Steinmetz's house George Gentrup gave me back the key and I opened the door. I then handed him back the key.

"There's another in the office," I said. "I can use it if I need to get back inside."

The house was the latest of numerous Bington houses where Steinmetz had lived. It was comfortable, but small, with two bedrooms, a medium-sized front room, an old-fashioned bath with a huge, claw-footed tub, and

an eat-in kitchen. I remembered the house hadn't cost
big bucks, but I also remembered that he'd spent some
money fixing it up to suit his needs. I'd liked his place
on the lake near Bington, but someone had come along
and offered him a good profit on it. He'd cannily sold it
and moved here.

One of the bedrooms had been turned into a study or
den. Steinmetz did his reading and writing there. It was
the only room I really knew and so I went there.

At first I couldn't get any indication whether anyone
had been inside the house. Maybe someone had, maybe
not. The study looked normal to me at first glance. His
old typewriter sat on its table and there were a few
sheets of paper near it. Rows of books seemed in order.
The morning paper for Wednesday was on the floor by
his chair. It came early in the morning, long before the
mail. Some opened mail, probably from Tuesday, was
on his desk. I riffled through it, but there was nothing.

My recollection was that the cleaning lady came once
a week, but I couldn't recall what day. Tuesday?
Wednesday?

She was an older lady, but still younger than Steinmetz. I remembered that Steinmetz had told me she'd
worked for him, off and on, for years. Maybe she'd
known Gail Marie. Maybe they'd kept in contact. I decided that when she turned up I wanted to talk to her.

I remembered that Steinmetz, at least at one time, had
kept a locked grey steel box of papers in the right bottom drawer of his desk. I'd seen him get things out of it
over the years. I slid the drawer open.

It wasn't there. I tried the other drawers. Still nothing of interest. I'd seen inside the box on several occa-
sions. He kept his personal papers there, insurance poli-
cies, car titles, deeds.

Maybe his will?

Perhaps he'd moved the box to some other area of the house. I went from study to bedroom and looked in drawers and closets there. Nothing. George Gentrup followed patiently behind.

"Someone's been inside the house," I said positively.

"What is it you're looking for?" George asked.

"A greyish metal box. He kept papers in it. I can't find it. He used to keep it in the right bottom drawer of his desk. It isn't there and it isn't here." I thought about it. "It's possible he got tired of keeping it here and rented himself a lockbox at the bank."

"Lockboxes cost money, Don."

"I know that."

"Which bank? I'll put in a call."

"He did most of his business with Ed Sturges at the main branch of the Trust Company, but I guess you could try them all."

I listened while George called all the banks in the area, even one across the river. Steinmetz had no lockboxes in the Bington area.

I telephoned my own office when Gentrup was done. I asked for and got Jake Bornstein, one of my partners who, being the managing partner, ran the office.

"Hah," he said, "you're back. That's good. Jo called and said you were off on a goose chase in the city to look for Steinmetz's daughter. I know how much you love the city so I wasn't expecting your return for a period of weeks."

"Try to hide your disappointment. I'll be in later. Do you know whether Steinmetz kept any kind of personal files around the office?"

"I don't know. When you get here we'll give her a

look. And I need to talk to you about the Ritzler damage case."

"Sure," I said, without much interest. "Anything going on around the office other than that?"

"Some doll, and I do mean doll, came in to see you about a divorce yesterday. P-r-e-t-t-y. I got the info from her, but she wasn't having any of me. She wants to see you in person. I suppose it's your charm. And there've been some telephone calls and some other people in to see you. They talked to me. But not Miss Prettypants."

Something came to me. "Jake, does Steinmetz have big money?"

He paused and then laughed. "I thought you knew."

"Nope. But someone's been inside his house and taken the metal box he kept his personal papers in and maybe other things I don't know about. I always thought Steinmetz had his judge's retirement and what he makes out of the office. Is there more?"

"Don, dear man, he's double loaded. Most people in town don't know it because he's always lived poor. I doubt he even spends his judge's retirement and he lives in that shack on Main Street when he could buy a palace. He's so tight he sold his place out on the lake, which he loved, when Henry Congress, his real estate pal, found him a big bucks buyer for it. He's switched from Jack Daniel's to Early Times, and those cigars he chews are cheap, cheap. He could buy and sell most of the people in this town and he could spill Jack Daniel's by the case."

I thought about that. "I never knew. He takes joy in sticking me for drinks and his clothes are seedy. He wears the doggiest golf clothes I've ever seen." I nodded to myself. "Do something for me. See what you can find of his around the office, anything personal or that looks

interesting. Hide it. I think there's a good chance someone's been inside his house and cleaned out what was
there. Maybe someone's already done the same in the
office."

"That could normally be, but not just now. When
was the last time you were in the office?"

"A couple of days ago, the day before Steinmetz had
his stroke. I was in early and left to go to court."

He laughed. "I've been talking about it for years, but
you've ignored me. Two days ago the painters and plas-
terers came when we closed the office at five. They've
been coming in both nights since, working a double
shift from five at night to nine in the morning. So, unless they broke in here before two days ago, no one
could easily have managed to take anything from the
office."

I was encouraged. "For once you've fumbled well."

"Wait'll you see your office. I thought about purple or
bright green, but then I got a little less conservative."

"How conservative?"

"Kind of an electric blue." He laughed wildly.

I rehung the phone while Jake was still laughing and
turned to George Gentrup. His thin, wise face was ex-
pressionless.

"If someone got what was here at the house then it's
doubtful they've gotten what's in the office. Jake's looking and I'll look some more." I thought for a long moment. "Maybe there ought to be some kind of special
guard on Steinmetz?"

"He has around-the-clock nurses."

"I mean like armed guards. Jake says he's got a lot of
money. Someone will get it when and if he dies."

"Surely he's got a will."

"My bet is he does, but it's not to be found here in his

house. If someone got the will, assuming there was one,
then who inherits with no will found?"

"Maybe . . . his heirs at law?"

"Right. You've just passed one minor section of the
state bar examination. So Steinmetz may be in danger if
the people who left the note control his daughter and
she's either his beneficiary by will or if he were to die
and no will be found."

"You think they might try to get Steinmetz while he's
in the hospital?"

"They might, and so, maybe, might others," I said,
not knowing for sure.

He nodded. "Okay. I'll send someone to the hospital
to watch his room," Gentrup said. "How about checking around your legal profession this afternoon and seeing if any of the local bar ever made a will for him?"

"I'll do it or have it done, but knowing Steinmetz, if
there's a will, he made it himself." I smiled and saw a
quick one appear in response on Gentrup's face. His
smiles somehow reminded me of opening a very small
switchblade, a quick widening and then, *flick*, closed.

Gentrup said, "Steinmetz is tight—tighter than jeans
on a sixteen-year-old."

"Why is he that way?" I asked, more curious than
interested.

"He grew up in a depression. By the time you and me
were born it was mostly over. My father told me there
were days when he was hungry and there was nothing
to eat. Bad times."

"Hold on to your hat, friend. Look around you and
see the street sleepers, the drunks, the druggies. It may
come again soon."

"Yeah."

FIVE

"Steinmetz's Memoirs" (manuscript) page 125: "Who cares what the place you practice in looks like? That's except for the I.R.S. And they want to see inside your safe deposit boxes also."

I DISCOVERED my office had been painted a decent light blue and looked reasonably presentable. The plaster in the ceiling where I'd counted the cracks when bored had been repaired. The workers had covered all while they worked. There were no paint stains and no bits of plaster to mar my inspection. Tarpaulins were leaned against the wall in a once vacant corner of my room. I looked the newly painted office over without any desire to go back to work. Sooner or later I knew I'd have to. I've found, down the years, that I have but minor tolerance for wills, contracts, and civil lawsuits. Sometimes, when there's nothing else to do, I manage to stomach civil practice without much enjoying it.

Jake sat behind his oversize desk and smiled up at me when I stopped at his door. Together we sniffed the odor of drying paint. His wall color was a medium grey.

"Steinmetz is doing okay," he said. "Leastways that was the word from the crew, including Doc Buckner, at coffee time this morning."

"Did you find anything of his around the office?"

"Two folders marked personal. No will, but there

was a list of stocks owned or once owned by Steinmetz. The list was prepared for him a while back by Tate Lockhart. Do you know Tate?"

The name Lockhart rang a small bell, but I shook my head.

"He's what passes for a big-time stockbroker around Bington. I talked to him a bit ago. He used to buy and sell for Steinmetz, but he said Steinmetz stopped being active, at least with him, a year or two ago. Tate told me that Steinmetz then had an assortment of blue chip stuff. He was reticent about values, but when I insisted he mentioned low seven figures."

"Jesus my all, Steinmetz's a millionaire. And him sticking me for drinks and driving that Ford more ancient than mine when he can't bum a ride with me or you."

"That's how he got to be a millionaire," Jake said, smiling. "He kept his dollars on interest and suckered us into buying for him."

"Why did he do that?"

Jake shrugged.

"Any sign of the whereabouts of the stock certificates?"

Jake shook his head. "No. And no will to be found. The list of securities is all stocks, no bonds, no bearer stuff. Steinmetz seemed more interested in growth stuff than he was in income. Tate said most of his stock dividends were eaten up in reinvestment programs. Steinmetz would only drag enough down to pay his taxes."

"A true believer in the American dream." I looked gloomily out Jake's office window. "He's got to have made a will. A lawyer just automatically would." I thought some on it. "Even if he didn't, the only way the stock can be sold, if Steinmetz dies, is by an estate administrator. That would be with his daughter inheriting all under the intestate succession laws."

"Steinmetz will make it again," Jake said, his voice as positive as a Rotarian predicting a good year in local sales. "Then we'll make sure he makes a new will and we'll get psychiatrists to be his witnesses so that there's no chance of breaking it. He's no spring chicken you know."

"That's true, even though his investments are for the future. Let's hope he does make it to maybe enjoy his dollars and spend a few on us for all he's stuck us for. He probably will live, because he's as tough as steak at a buck a pound." I smiled to myself, remembering past times. Steinmetz had suckered us and parlayed raveled shirts, gravy ties, and out-of-style suits into free drinks, dinners, and gratis transportation. "One way or another we've got to get even with him for the years he sponged off us."

"How lucid was he when you first saw him at the hospital?" Jake asked seriously.

"I thought he knew what he wanted, but it was hard for him to communicate those wants to me. He was weak and Doc Buckner ran me out quickly. What I got for sure out of the Judge is that he wanted me to look for his daughter. Find her."

"And you've not located her yet?"

I told him what had happened north and how far along I was. He listened intently.

"So now Gentrup has his people guarding Steinmetz at the hospital and the two of you think there might be some attempt on Steinmetz's life for his money?"

"Could be. I got to thinking on that earlier. If they wanted him dead why not do him in first off instead of leaving a note?"

Jake looked thoughtful. "Maybe they thought they could get some easy money out of him and when that didn't work out they are now doing some more figuring? Or maybe they didn't want to do him in until they knew exactly what his will said."

"Could be either way. Plan one fails. It can't work because Steinmetz has a stroke. They get his will out of the house and find out that his daughter's cut out or mostly cut out of it. Plan two then becomes the alternative with the will gone. Thing is that they're probably not sure the will is gone. Let's assume his will did leave his daughter something. They then kill Steinmetz and wait to see if a will's probated. Steinmetz wouldn't be the first man to get scragged for his dollars. Remember the Huggards?"

Jake nodded. Elbert Huggard had been in his eighties when bad things began to happen to him. Now he was an area legend. His much younger wife and his two boys by a previous marriage had combined in a conspiracy for cash. They'd fed him arsenic for a time. When he had his first major sickness from the arsenic it came in town, farmer-style, on a Saturday. So he'd wound up in the Bington hospital where he'd refused to peacefully die. In fact he'd soon gotten well enough to go back home. The wife and sons had then hit him with a baseball bat and dropped him out of a second-story window in the Huggard mansion. Unfortunately a bird-watching neighbor had witnessed the fall and the causation thereof. All three younger Huggards were now serving long sentences. Elbert Huggard had survived the fall and in the early spring I'd seen him out plowing his acreage. Rumors said that he'd taken up with his new housekeeper, a church-going widow who seemed spry and was into clog dancing.

Jake asked slyly, "Then you're spending full-time looking for Steinmetz's daughter and her pals?"

"No. I'm also representing Stanley Willetts and I'm supposed to be looking into his murder situation."

"Full-time?" Jake asked again.

"Not yet. But I do want to get back to him the first of the week and I may spend some time on it over the weekend."

Jake smiled triumphantly. "Way to figure. You'll get peanuts from the court for representing Willetts and nothing from Steinmetz. So pull yourself up a chair. I've got some things to talk to you about. Civil trials. Money stuff, where I can use you. You aren't the best lawyer around, but sometimes you commit some cunning treacheries in court."

For the moment I gave up trying to escape.

Office routine caught up with me. I looked over thick civil files which had been placed on my desk by Jake or a secretary. There were, as there'd always been since the early lean days had passed, things to do, busy work. I plunged in like a springtime swimmer into an ice-cold creek.

At three-thirty Jake came to my door, saw I was immersed in civil crap, and grinned in at me approvingly.

"One of our efficient secretaries, at my whispered request, phoned the lovely lady with the divorce problem —the one who insisted on waiting to see you while you were away. Your prospective client's now in the reception room." He rolled his eyes suggestively. "And she's something extra special just as I earlier reported. If Jo wandered in and saw her in your office discussing things she might make you forego all domestic relations work in the future."

"Stop drooling. You're ruining the hall rug. Have someone show her back. Then close your door and don't eavesdrop."

"Not on your life," he said. He went away.

I waited curiously. Jake's idea of female beauty and mine sometimes clashed. A secretary brought Jake's dream back.

She was special. I think they make a few like her every decade or so. Each one's different, but they're all a part of the same club. Some of them wind up in show business, some of them marry millionaires, and some become courtesans. All have men falling in flames around them for all of their lives.

She had midnight hair that curled and was full of life and lights. She wore a white nurse's uniform that made me wish I was unwell. It fit her cunningly. Most nurse's uniforms fit nurses like they fit hangers, but this one fit. She was tall and slim and her legs seemed ten feet long and all of the woman fell together scrupulously. Her eyes were the shade of blue I imagined when I dreamed in winter of early spring flowers. Her lips were delicately carved and touched with red. Her nose was both haughty and cute. I decided she could stop a war or start one.

"You'd asked to see me," I said, keeping myself calm and collected. "I'm Don Robak."

"Yes," she admitted. Her voice was created to be a part of her, deep and smoky.

"Sit down," I said with too much enthusiasm. "Tell me what I can do to help you?"

"I want a divorce and there's a problem. My husband's a Mexican citizen. He's left and apparently has fled back to Mexico like two months back. I've not heard from him directly since he ran off on me."

"Do you own any property, real or personal, together?"

"Kind of. He took everything he could carry with him. He cleaned out our joint savings before he left. There's one exception. There's a car in both our names. I think he'd have taken it also if he could have found it, but I'd driven it to work, had a minor problem on the way, and left it at a garage near work the day he cleaned the rest of the stuff out." She shook her head. "It must have ruined him leaving the car behind. I found the place where he got a rental when they sent me the bill."

"How much joint savings?"

"About thirty thousand dollars," she said without visible anger. "Some of it was mine, but most of it was his."

"What kind of car?"

She smiled and made my day seem brighter. "A one-year-old Mercedes 500 series, low miles, and paid for. It was my wedding gift, but I found, when I looked at the title in the glove compartment after he was gone, that Ramon had registered it in both our names."

"So you have possession of both the car and car title now?"

She nodded. "The title's in my lockbox at the Trust Bank. Let's say I took some precautions to keep the car safe after Ramon took his leave. Earlier this month a man called. He said he was calling for my husband and he demanded the car. He said if I didn't give it back that bad things might happen."

"Bad things of what nature?"

"He sounded mean. He mentioned replevin for one thing."

If there was no money owed to a dealer or a bank I doubted

*anyone could manage to replevin the car, even if they did repre-
sent Ramon. It seemed logical law anyway.*

"Where are you keeping this car now?"

She shifted her long legs beautifully and I was properly awed. "Do you really want to know?"

I slid a bit deeper into my chair. "I guess I don't. Is it
somewhere your caller can't and won't find it?"

"Yes. It's not here in Bington. I've got it stored safely
in another town with friends that Ramon never met
and that he doesn't know about. I'm driving a rental
until things are straightened out. In the divorce I'd like
you to try to get the car for me. That way I can sell it. I
then can get enough money to start a new savings and
buy myself a cheaper car. Do you think you could get
the car for me?"

"I would try very hard. No children?"

She blushed just a little. "Hey, we were only married
for about a year. No children and none expected." She
looked me over questioningly. "I wanted you because
you were highly recommended. One of the doctors at
the hospital said you were tough and wouldn't scare or
sell out. I think there's a good chance that my sweet
Ramon was maybe into drugs and might have used the
Mercedes to transport them. I think he might have gone
back south or somewhere with someone else's drugs and
that someone now wants the car to get repaid for what
Ramon stole."

"Why do you think that?"

"There's some good reasons. The man who called also
had a Spanish accent. He wasn't pleasant with me and
he seemed very angry at Ramon. He didn't believe me
when I told him I didn't know Ramon's whereabouts.
He said he'd find both Ramon and the car. I told him
about the bank account being lifted and he got a little

more reasonable, but he still said I had to give him the car. He made it sound like it might be unhealthy for me if I didn't give it to him."

"What did you tell him?"

"I told him to go haunt a used car lot."

"Have you heard from him since?"

"No. I moved to another apartment. I think maybe he, or maybe someone helping Ramon, has me located again by now. There might be someone watching me. I now live in a small apartment near the university with two other nurses. We work different shifts; the other two work days, and me nights. It's safe there. I've asked my neighbors to call the police if they hear anything funny from the apartment when I'm alone." She shook her head. "The walls are like paper in those apartments and one neighbor is an elderly lady in a wheelchair who claims she can hear me breathing. She never goes anywhere." She shrugged. "I guess I'm as safe there as anywhere I could be."

I considered it and nodded.

"Should I maybe call you if anyone tries to get in?" she asked, smiling at me.

I was tempted, but I said, "Call the police first and then call me. How about the car? Did you check it over to make certain there aren't any drugs hidden in it?"

"I did that. I've got a detective friend, female, who's an expert in that area. If there are any drugs, we couldn't find them. Neither could the two drug-sniffing dogs she borrowed. They just acted bored."

I nodded and decided it was time to put down the necessaries for filing a dissolution of marriage. Jake had said he'd gotten them, but I decided to get them again. I took some notes for the petition. His name was Ramon Sanchez and hers was Stella, previous name Stella Ann

Brown. They'd married in Capitol City a year before and she'd moved on to Bington three months back, when he'd left her. Enough to satisfy residency, both state and Mojeff County. Enough to file and ask for a dissolution of marriage and a property settlement with the car as her part of it. And enough so that I could convince Judge Harner, when I put her in front of him and he was properly dazzled (as he would be), that she truly deserved the Mercedes. I'd also alert him, when I filed the case, that there was another spurious claim to the car and that someone might try to run a replevin in front of him asking for an order without hearing. But we'd leave the car in the other city until these things came to pass, so even if the judge forgot, there'd be no findable property for someone with an order until I could get a hearing questioning that order.

I asked more questions. I listened to Stella as she answered. I tried to figure out her ancestry, but I couldn't fathom it. She looked English or Scotch or maybe Irish with a touch from somewhere else. The Brown name meant nothing. I thought maybe she'd been married before Ramon, but it wasn't something I needed to know for a dissolution of marriage. The net results of Stella were all lovely sums.

When we were done I was reluctant for it to end, but I had enough information, and keeping her here, with Jake slavering away in his room, meant having to tell him why.

"The papers will be ready in the morning if you want to sign them then. If I need to reach you for something I've missed, where do I call?"

"Best place is the hospital, night shift, but that's tonight only this week. I was about to take a short trip and visit some people. I'll be back in when I return. Maybe the first of the week."

"Are you visiting the people who have your Mercedes?"

"No, not them. Not until you get it for me and I get it sold. Some other friends."

I picked up her information sheet.

"We've got a member of this law firm over in the hospital in intensive care."

She nodded. "I know. I heard about him. He used to be the circuit judge. In the asking I also got told about you by a nice doctor, who's also a nice *married* doctor."

"How's Steinmetz doing?"

"I'd know if he was bad, but probably not otherwise. I work the emergency room. Lots of action." She got up from her chair. I smelled the odor of good soap and a fragrance that was partly subtle perfume, partly woman.

I eased back in my own chair. Jo was also lovely. Jo was safe and mine. I'd lost one wife who'd divorced me when I was in law school because she'd found someone who, she'd thought, could give her a better, more comfortable life. He couldn't now and it was comforting to see them at high school reunions. He was ten years older than me and he was both heavy and bald. He wheezed when he talked and his ties were always undone at the neck. I could sit at the reunion table and watch my ex-wife's cold eyes contemplating me and a world that might have been. I always wore my best suit to reunions and drank wine or martinis. Carefully. And, had there been no Jo, I'd not have given my ex-wife a second look.

Even if the invitation was there from Stella Sanchez, and maybe it was, I didn't want to take chances by start-

ing something. It's easy to be both unhappy and a fool,
easy to screw things up. Yet the urge was strong.

She watched me and I thought she was puzzled. She
knew her power, she knew I was interested, but so far
I'd not made the moves she expected.

"The papers will be ready tomorrow or whenever
you're ready to sign them." I explained the filing fees
and she got out her purse and paid me in hundreds.

I escorted her to the office front door and let her go. I
watched her drive away. Her rental was a used Mus-
tang. I watched it out of sight. I saw no one following
her. She was so lovely, I thought that everyone she approached in her apartment house would look out for
her.

From his office, when I returned to mine, Jake
watched me. He was grinning like a goblin at a Hallow-
een party.

"Whoopee," he said. "You are either strong, sick, or
tired."

"All," I answered.

The land across the bridge and river was not a well-
known land to me, but it was the place where Mrs.
Milton lived. Crossing the bridge was like going from
one country to another rather than just going into an
adjoining state. Down the years I'd made a few friends
across the bridge, but I called none of them on this middle afternoon, having decided to see what I could learn
by a quick trip on my own after Stella Sanchez departed
my office.

At a grocery store in the "downtown" of the tiny
village across the bridge I got directions to Mrs.
Milton's house from a curious, bespectacled store-
keeper. He carried his Pepsi to his front door and

checked my car and license plate as I drove back past his place from his side parking lot.

The house was supposed to be down the main highway a mile and a half, left off the highway and onto a gravel road, then up the first dirt road to the right a few hundred feet.

I drove the Ford LTD that way. Farmers worked their tobacco plants under a warm sun. Ladies in sun hats weeded in vegetable gardens or watered flowers. Now and then someone would wave to me, perhaps because I was driving slow. I waved back. I was maybe three miles from Bington, in another state, but things had slowed and gone backward twenty years. I had the windows of the Ford down and the air smelled of new green growth and of the ancient river that lay near.

I found the gravel road and then the dirt road and proceeded up it. The dirt road ended in the front yard of a small, weathered house with a porch. Behind the house a barn was decaying, folding in upon itself, ten degrees right. I parked. The house needed paint. A Dodge Ram truck sat ahead of me in the drive. It was dented and so dirty I couldn't guess its year. Up close I could see it had a rack in the streaked rear window with a rifle and a shotgun in the rack. Its rear bumpers held obscene stickers. I succeeded in not blushing.

I tapped on the door, but no one came. I knocked loudly with no results.

I walked to the far end of the porch and looked around the corner of the house. No one.

I stepped off the porch and walked all the way around the house. By the time I got back to the porch a man stood just off it watching me. He was a large man, too big to be called just fat, three hundred plus pounds, maybe six foot four.

"I'm looking for Mrs. Milton," I said.

"For what?" he asked. He was heavily bearded and I could read no change in his expression. He was surely thirty, maybe forty. His beard had a few touches of grey.

"She works for one of my law partners in Bington."

He nodded without any discernible meaning. "That'd be old Judge Steinmetz. I heared he was in the hospital and about ready to go to the bone pile. I don't care about him, but I hope he took good care of my mom in his will. He owes her lots."

"Mrs. Milton's your mother?"

"Yeah."

"Judge Steinmetz had a stroke, but he's doing okay now," I said softly. "I came over to find your mother. I was wondering if your mother ever saw anyone hanging around the judge's house when she was cleaning it? Did she ever say anything like that to you?"

"Not me." He scratched his head with a sausage-size finger. "Just now she's gone off somewhere to visit for a while."

"Did you ever hear your mother saying anything about the judge's daughter, Gail Marie Steinmetz?"

He shook his head.

"You know when she'll be back?"

He shrugged. "Who knows. She's related to about half the people in the five counties around here. She comes and she goes like she pleases and without telling me." He stopped, looked down at the ground, and pawed it with a size fourteen shoe. "You tell that old judge that he owes my mom for lots of things she did for him and he ain't paid for. The few bucks a week he gave her until he fired her won't pay for all she did for him and he knows it. If she has to sue him she damn well will."

"Steinmetz fired her?"

"That's what she said. A few weeks ago after lots of years of hard work. Hired someone else younger and prettier."

"I'd like to talk to your mother. Tell her that or, better, tell me where I can find her."

He looked me up and down. "You're one nosy lawyer bastard. If I knew where she was at I'd not tell you. Best get back across the river now and tell that damned old judge what I said. He better take care of my mom and pay her what he owes. He don't do that and I'll come see him if he don't up and die by hisself first." He took a threatening step toward me. "And now talk's over. You move out, mister."

I nodded. I was a visitor. He had a right to be there. I did not. I walked slowly back to the car and started it up. He stood in the shade of the sagging porch and watched me balefully down the road.

I wasn't unsatisfied with the conversation. I now knew that Steinmetz had fired Mrs. Milton.

I thought I ought to tell George Gentrup about that.

SIX

"Steinmetz's Memoirs" (manuscript) page 201: "I've been a success as a lawyer even though I'm not much good in court. I suppose it's because I am quite a decent golfer."

FROM THE BRIDGE I drove directly to the Bington police station and waited a while to see George Gentrup. The air conditioner in the desk area was installed in a small window and was insufficient, except in sound, to do the job. I sat in a hard chair and sweated until George came to the desk area and led me back to his office, where things were quiet and cool.

"I doubt your police people can hear the phone over the air conditioner noise out there."

He tapped a pencil on his desk. "They can hear the phone. I've reported the problem to the city council. Unlike you, Robak, I think they favor the idea of police officers sitting in the booking area and sweating it out."

"It's very comfortable here in your office," I said, smiling idly.

"The privilege of rank," he said. "And my air conditioner is too big to fit their window. We tried." He cocked his head and looked me over. "Why, I do believe you've broken yourself into a nasty sweat, dear Robak. Might I suggest a quick journey home, a shower, and some Right Guard. Also use it, if you can remember, on your left side."

I glanced at my watch and shook my head. "In about half an hour I go to play at golf. After a hole or two no one will believe I'm fresh from a shower, so why bother? Besides, sometimes it's fun to feel clammy."

He nodded at my wisdom. "It seems I've found your area of freakiness. What brings you here?"

I told him about my trip across the river. He listened with no more than minor interest.

"Is there something you want me to do?" he asked when I had finished.

I shrugged. "I thought it valuable to learn that Steinmetz had fired Mrs. Milton, that she's not at home, and that her overgrown son insists that Steinmetz owes Mrs. Milton dollars. A desire for money sometimes leads to evil deeds."

"Is it that you're thinking Mrs. Milton could possibly be involved with the ladies from Capitol City?"

"Could be."

"Across the bridge is out of my jurisdiction."

I remembered the size of Mrs. Milton's son, the rifle and shotgun in the rear window of his truck. *Redneck. Act first, think later.*

"I think it might be good to locate her. Who knows— maybe she might tell us something about Steinmetz's daughter."

He thought on it and then nodded. "It's interesting, but why do I always feel that I'm spending too much of my job time working for you?"

"For Steinmetz," I corrected.

"While you rush around wasting the county's time in yet another murder case," he continued, ignoring my answer. "Would you like me to furnish you and let you carefully read a printout of Stanley Willetts's record?"

"I've seen it and read it. It's long. That's about all I have seen so far. No eyeball witnesses and my client denies the dirty deed. I've yet to do much checking on Mr. Willetts. I have, as I'm now reporting to you, been doing some things to try to find Steinmetz's daughter."

He looked up at the ceiling. "I hate lawyers, and your tugging at my apron strings doesn't cause that hate to abate one iota, but the sheriff across the bridge owes me a few. I shall call him and ask him to go past the house and maybe question this son of Mrs. Milton's. Then maybe I'll get back to you." He held up a hand. "Just don't ask me to be a character witness for Stan the Man when you try to screw that one up in court or out."

"Agreed." I looked at my watch. "I've time for an iced tea or a cold cola before I must head for the links and become athletic. Shall we walk down to the drugstore?"

He smiled his quick, grim smile. "Not today. Too much to do before I can leave."

I got up.

"Besides, there's my reputation to consider," he added.

Around five I drove to the country club. I put on golf gear in the locker room and met Jo on the first tee, where we played nine warm holes with a married pair, the Schwinns. He was loud and high fortyish in age, a hard-sell realtor, handsome in a florid way. He kept surveying Jo and ignoring his wife, who seemed not to notice, but probably did.

Jo, being a very neat lady, was also an observant one. She bubbled friendlily to the wife and was cool and short with the realtor, who was obtuse enough to treat her comments as small jokes. He laughed his way through the nine jolly holes. Now and then he'd nudge me when something came along he thought was particularly a knee slapper. I restrained myself and didn't nudge him back. It was difficult.

We finished before seven and I returned to the men's locker room. I showered short hot and then long cold, and felt better when I went upstairs. A Thursday buffet dinner awaited, meat loaf, green beans, and mashed potatoes, plus lots of fresh tomatoes and lettuce.

Before having at it I bought Jo a very tall gin and tonic which I knew she'd sip for an hour. For myself I got a V.O. and branch, plus a large glass of water and ice on the side. I sipped the first cautiously and drank the second.

The realtor came up from the basement and loudly demanded the right to pay for our drinks, since we'd had the better score, but I'd already paid and so I declined politely. I got a frown which put me in my place.

"I never seem to see your name on deeds or mortgages, so how do you manage to survive?" he asked aggressively, smiling only a little.

"I spend a small amount of my time filing lawsuits against people, but most of it I use defending the local criminal element. I have lots of friends who are professionals in crime." I smiled as thinly as I could. "Right now, some of them tell me, there appears to be a lot of land fraud things going on around Bington and out in the county. I've been researching into that all this week. God knows what'll happen when it all hits the streets and we take it to Herman Leaks. My people will, of course, demand immunity and get it."

He looked me over, not sure whether I was kidding. I

kept a straight face while he stirred his martini vigor-
ously and searched his soul. Other golfers came up from
the basement and the barroom began to fill up. Jo appeared from the ladies dressing room and I gave her the
gin and tonic.

The realtor turned to the man on the other side of
him for a time and then wandered away from the bar,
still unsure, but worried now.

"How did you manage to get rid of him?" Jo asked,
impressed. "I thought we were stuck with him at least
through dinner. His wife's nice, but he's an ass."

I explained.

"You nasty devil," she said, smiling at me nicely and
raising my temperature. "But how do you ever expect
to improve your business and get to do good things like
deeds and contracts if you tell people awful lies?"

I nuzzled her a bit, being sedate about it. The bar was
crowded, people wedged in tight, having what was supposed to be small town fun.

I said in Jo's ear, "He didn't want to do business with
me. He was, I think, hopeful of working out some kind
of arrangement with you."

She nodded. "He said once, when you weren't close,
that he had a house he'd like to show me. I wonder how
many times he's gotten a response to that?"

"Probably lots. Not much to do in warm weather
time in Bington."

And so it went. We drank and talked to old friends
and then ate the buffet dinner. The realtor soon decided
I had to be kidding and worked again at being friendly
with Jo.

After the festivities began to subside we went out
into the parking lot. Jo's aunt, anxious to care for son

Joe, had brought wife Jo to the club. My Ford was our
one car.

In the dark parking lot, as others tooted their horns at
us and left, I sought the Ford.

I looked long.

I looked hard.

I one-on-oned every car in the parking lot and then I
did it again.

The Ford was gone.

On Friday morning I checked my desk. My file on
Gail Marie Steinmetz lay there where I'd left it. Under
it was my file on the Willetts murder case where I'd also
left it. I'd thought maybe both files were in the car and
that was why it had been stolen.

Not so.

On Friday my stunning divorce-seeker didn't appear,
but then she'd said she'd be out for the weekend, so I
thought little about it.

I did call the hospital employment office. Yes, she was
working there, but she had taken time off and wouldn't
return until Monday.

On Friday I read over my file on the Willetts case.
The information, drawn up in Herman Leaks's pedan-
tic style, charged that Stanley Willetts had struck Ruby
Geneva Willetts multiple blows with a sledge hammer
and then and thereby caused her to die. There was a list
of witnesses which was slender and appeared to be
mostly those who'd heard threats or seen Stanley on or
around his wife's home (and I found by checking the
title that it truly was her home, not his or in joint
names) on the day she'd died. I found out that Honey
Willetts had worked as a waitress and that her last employment had been in March. I found she had no driv-

er's license and had no vehicle registered in her name. I
looked over Stanley's record again. It was three pages
long on the NCIC printout. *Impressive.*
That used up Friday.

On Saturday morning, driving a tiny toy Japanese
rental truck, I journeyed south and west of Bington. I
followed the old county and river road that ran near the
edge of the wide, muddy river. I slowed now and then,
looking for a place I'd been long before. My plan was to
spend the morning looking further for Gail Marie, and
the afternoon, if nothing got complicated about Gail
Marie, interviewing the witnesses in the Willetts case.

My Ford remained stolen. George Gentrup's ex-
pressed belief that a kid had taken it for a joyride had
not been the answer. The Ford had vanished and was
now on the hotsheet in forty-nine states.

"What was in it?" George had asked.

"Not much." There hadn't been, to the best of my
recollection. Some items in the glove compartment,
maps and the like, minor tools. An ice scraper. An um-
brella that wasn't much good.

The picture of Gail Marie I'd taken from the album
I'd discovered in Steinmetz's house was in the office
case file. I now had it beside me on the passenger side of
the Toyota along with my file on State vs. Stanley Willetts. Two birds with a single stone for Saturday.

The river road was rough, part gravel, part potholed
asphalt. Each spring the river washed out some of it as
it rose and fell. Each summer county highway workers
rescued what was left and repaired what was taken.

Saturday had dawned fine weatherwise after big late-
night rains Friday after we were home. The thunder
and lightning had brought Joe to our bedroom. It

wasn't that he was afraid, he'd said, but he sure liked to be around other people when there was thunder and lightning. I remembered I had also, when I was a child.

The river was calm and muddy, but soon it would be boating weather, drift or no drift.

I passed fishing shacks and some better houses. The river and the road above it were vacation areas for many. For those who liked water and could tolerate the never-ending rise, fall, and sometimes flood, it was home. People still valued its banks and built homes along them no matter how many times they were forced away and had to return to partly drowned houses.

What I was looking for was on the other side of the road, away from the river, out of the flood zone.

I finally located the private road I sought. A sign on a tree alerted me. It read, "No Trespassing." The sign was new, the road old and worn. I turned between trees on negligible remaining gravel and avoided the road center where there was a puddle that looked like it was deep enough to drown both me and my rental Toyota. I then stayed to the high side of the road for a time. Even there it was heavy going, but the truck made slow progress and soon brought me to where I could find decent purchase in the middle, as the private road rose away from the river and the public road that lay beside it.

Half a mile up from the river road there was a large, old house. It was built of brick and stone and must have once been very patrician. Now it sat in fading splendor, Victorian in style, three stories high. There was a good barn behind it. Someone had planted flowers in beds around the house and they grew in wild profusion, intermixed, without regard for balance, but still spring lovely. I had my driver's window rolled down and I smelled the flowers and trees as I drew close.

I knew the owner of the farm although we weren't close friends. Once, five or six years back, state police had raided the Victorian farmhouse believing marijuana was being cultivated under hot lights inside. It wasn't. Not much in the way of any evidence had been found, but the state boys, in their search, had found some drug paraphernalia, a substantial amount of smokable pot, and a small amount of cocaine. They'd then gleefully arrested everyone in sight for felony possession, happy to have something to show for their abortive effort. Those arrested had been four in number, the owner of the farm and three buxom friends, all female.

I pulled up close to the front porch and blew my horn. I didn't desire to get out and go exploring. I thought it was possible that the house occupant or occupants might blow large pieces of me into smaller pieces with shotguns.

The horn made a sorry sound. Nothing happened and so I blew it again, three times.

A woman came to the door. She stood watching me from inside the screen. She was holding something and I thought it was a rifle or a shotgun. I opened my door and got carefully out of the car keeping my hands always in sight.

The woman set the gun down, opened her screen door, and emerged.

"Robak, you old bastard," she said. She smiled at me and nodded her head. She was a strong-looking woman and appeared to be around my age, but I knew she was in her sixties. Her name was Sylvia Robinette. She was a mean, independent, openly practicing, completely defiant lesbian. She hated everything male, and that included me, even though I'd helped her once.

She came gracefully down her stone porch steps and

grabbed me around the waist and wrestled me about for a moment good naturedly. She was very strong. Inside her house I knew she had exercise machines and used them religiously. I knew also that she ran often and well, and that she swam in the treacherous Ohio River even in the winter.

"What brings you out this way?" she asked, releasing me.

"I need to talk to you about something," I said.

She smiled some more. "Last time I saw you was the day the circuit judge granted your motion to suppress, when the state pukes had me and mine in a lot of drug trouble."

I looked momentarily up at the door of her house and then quickly back at Sylvia before she caught me at it. Someone else listened inside the shadows. I'd caught a small movement across the door.

"They made the search warrant out wrong," I explained. "It was for pot you were growing and not pot you were smoking. A technicality maybe, but enough to suppress what they got out of your house."

"Made that prim, silly-looking prosecutor mad as hell, I remember," she said, relishing our single shared triumph.

"It did do that. Do you remember the judge we had on it? Judge Steinmetz?"

She nodded. "I remember him. I saw he got beat a couple of years later, but I made a point of getting to the polls and voting for him. Crusty old bastard, but he was fair. Not many men are, these days, to people who believe as I do."

"He got beat like you said and went off the bench. He became a part of my law firm. Now he's in the hospital and I'm trying to find his daughter."

She waited awarely, not smiling at me now.

"This daughter was living, until a few weeks ago, with some other ladies up on Emmetson Boulevard in Capitol City."

"I've been in a couple of places on Emmetson, some bars. Are you trying to say what I think you're trying to say?"

"I am. I think his daughter's a lesbian or is, at least, living with someone who is one. By the time I got to where she'd lived up there, she and her friends had moved on, probably to come back here. I thought maybe you might have heard something about her." I handed her the picture and she looked at it briefly and gave it back.

"I need to find her for her father," I said. "He's had a bad stroke."

She stood silent for a long moment and then shook her head. "I'd like to be of help, Don. Believe me when I say I would. But I can't and won't. I don't do anything to cause me or those like me problems." She held up a hand and stopped my reply. "I'll pass on the word through the local sisterhood. I'll tell it around that you want to find her, that her father wants to find her. *That's all.*"

"Okay," I said. "Thank you for that." I looked out at her fields. They lay fallow. Nothing now grew on the farm. Nothing had since Sylvia bought the place. Sylvia had inherited money, a trust fund that paid her some income, and she used that to live. The farm was for her privacy, for her retreat, and not for cultivation.

A minority of the gay ones, male and female, hate heterosexuals. We made them into second-class citizens and held them in contempt for thousands of years. Most societies made them hide their sexual preferences in dark places or suffer in the open. We passed statutes and set work rules. Gay was evil. Being gay meant jail sentences and getting beaten up, without recourse, by "normals." Gay meant scorn and bad jokes, poor jobs, or no jobs at all.

Now, in the new light of our present society, the gays march, they file lawsuits, and they hold us in a curious reverse contempt. Some of them are bright and gifted, some of us aren't. They have a legend that they tell among their inner groups, a legend some believe: their ways are the ways of the future.

I doubted it would be that way, seeing as how it was hard for them to procreate, but my own life has made me tolerant of what others desire to believe. If they wanted that belief for their hope of salvation, it was all right with me.

I walked back and opened the Toyota's door.

"Must be lonely out here for you this time of year," I said.

She watched me with no warmth at all. Camaraderie was over. I'd once represented her and won for her in court. She'd paid me and that was that.

"It's lonely, Robak," she answered civilly. "I want to see someone then I have to go into town. I'm too old for the fast scene, but that's about all there is these days and it's a careful, make that a very careful, scene now. I guess I'm too old to stop. No one for me now. One day soon there may be again." She smiled philosophically. "Someone to warm me in my old age."

"Sure, Sylvia."

Her eyes went hard. "I wouldn't do as much as I'm doing now if you hadn't done something once for me. Don't come back here again without an invitation.

That's a warning. And I mean it. I've heard stories
about you and I don't want you around here."

"All right and thanks again," I said. I got in and
started the Toyota's motor. I gave Sylvia a wave and
drove back down the road.

I found a good place half a mile up the river road, a
place where I could park and hide the Toyota behind
trees. I left it and slogged back to Sylvia's farm. Once on
the farm I stayed behind trees and managed to get close
to the big house and barn.

By then my shoes looked like two mud balls.

The place I found to watch from was a small copse of
weeds, bramble bushes, vines, and gum trees. New
leaves and stickers and gumballs had already grown
fully and I parted the combination and made a small
hole so I could see the farmhouse and barn from my
place of concealment.

A pair of robins watched me from above, interested
in my movements. Insects tentatively explored me.
Three red squirrels scared away the birds and played
tag in the trees. My small world smelled of weeds and
grass.

I waited patiently, watching the house. I grew hungry. No one came to the house. No one left.

Behind Sylvia's house the hills that bordered the river
rose up sharply. Once there'd been a medium-sized
town to the south along the river, but the years of rising
and falling water had finally worn out the town after
the monster flood of 1937. Now all that remained were a
few foundations of homes long gone and old rusting
railroad tracks. Those rail tracks led to a railroad cut
that ran up the hill behind Sylvia's house. I'd been up
and down it often. I could see it now, a slash in the hill.

Until five or ten years ago a tourist train had run down the cut once a month, but even that had now stopped.

In the middle of the afternoon, after I'd grown very weary of watching, Sylvia exited her front door. She stood at the top of the porch steps and looked around for a long time. I stayed motionless.

If she saw me or thought I was out there she gave no indication. She whistled some kind of signal.

A young woman, answering the whistle, came out onto the porch and joined Sylvia. Together the pair walked toward the barn, rolled a big door back, and drove away in a recent vintage Jeep station wagon. *Grocery shopping? Going to town to call on friends?*

I watched them drive away. When I was certain they were gone I still sat warily for a long time. The bugs kept biting me.

The woman who'd accompanied Sylvia had not been Steinmetz's daughter. She'd been white, young, and pretty in a doll-like way. I thought it was possible, but not probable, that she might be the third tenant of the Emmetson apartment in Capitol City.

Sylvia had tried to give me the impression she was alone in the house. Maybe it was because she believed that her affairs weren't my business. Maybe it was something else. She'd told me not to return and she'd been very positive in the telling.

The house beckoned. If the station wagon returned I could escape when I heard them coming, hide on the far side of the barn while they parked, then make a run up the railroad cut to the hilltop far above Sylvia's house with excellent hope of success. I decided on the cut if I was caught short and had to run after they'd seen me. On top of the cut the land was wild. There were the remains of limestone deposits, the beginning of the

Madison Outcrop, which had played out as commer-
cially usable in the sixties. There were old quarries full
of heaped, jagged stones and cold water. There were
sinkholes and small caves. Sometimes I ran up there,
but it was no place even to walk after dark. I knew the
area without truly knowing it.

I waited for a longer time. Trespassing on another's
land was technically a crime, entering a house not your
own was a more serious one, but I'd done other things
not completely legal in my checkered career. Steinmetz
needed to find his daughter and my looking for her had
stirred my curiosity enough so that I was willing to take
minor chances. I didn't care what Sylvia thought or
what Sylvia wanted. I now had no more loyalty to her
than she had to me.

I moved carefully, staying behind tree and bush cover
where I could. I stayed away from the road area in the
front of the house and made my approach first to the
barn and then, in a short run, to the rear of the house.

I wiped my shoes as well as I could in the grass and
then went up double steps to the porch. The back porch
door was unlocked.

The solid wood back door that might have allowed
entrance into the house was locked. I tried it with the
intent to enter if it were unlocked. I backed off a step
when it refused to yield and bent and examined the
lock. It was too complicated for me to try to tinker with
and it seemed stout enough to resist force.

I leaned against the back door and put my ear to the
upper panel of wood. I could hear something, an odd
sound, from inside.

I exited the back porch and saw that I'd left mud
tracks behind. I went back and tried my handkerchief
on them with small results. Too much mud, too little

handkerchief. I gave up and moved on around the house. At a side window I could look in and see a sitting room with hallway door open. I decided that either Sylvia or her companion had forgotten a television set and left it on. *Or someone else was inside and was watching a movie or other program.*

A piano played softly and a man sang. I couldn't make it out and then I could. The song was "As Time Goes By." *Casablanca.*

I tried looking in other windows, but they belonged to downstairs rooms where the inner hall doors were closed.

I saw nothing of interest.

The sounds of *Casablanca* had to be coming from one of the upper floors.

I went to the front porch and tried the front door. It also was locked.

From far away I heard a sound. I thought it could be the station wagon returning. I listened intently. I heard it turn in and accelerate to escape the mud.

There was time. I didn't have to go up the hill beyond the house. Instead I fled back to my prior hiding place. I made it easily and watched Sylvia's Jeep wagon as I hunkered down deep in my thorn bushes.

Sylvia and unidentified friend exited the barn after parking. This time they left the barn door open behind them. They returned to the house. I heard them laughing and chattering together as they used a key and opened the front door of the house.

For the rest of the long afternoon I waited and watched. Stanley Willetts and his problems about his deceased wife would have to wait.

Nothing.

When it was almost dark the lights began to come on

in the house. Someone, and I thought from the shape at the windows that it was the girl who'd accompanied Sylvia, drew thick drapes upstairs and downstairs. One light came on for a moment on the third floor, but it also vanished quickly behind drapes.

I approached the barn carefully and went inside it. There was still enough light for me to see that only Sylvia's Jeep wagon was parked in the barn. On the walls there were some old rusty farm tools hung on nails, hoes, rakes, a scythe. It had been a long time since they'd been used.

I stayed in the shadows and walked on back to the river road to the place where I'd hidden the Toyota.

SEVEN

"Steinmetz's Memoirs" (manuscript) page 146: "When you speak of alternate life-styles, then alternate to what? In other words who's doing what to whom with which?"

TWIGGENS TWINKLE CLUB BAR AND GRILLE was out near the university in an area that had once been large, expensive homes until the tornado of 1975. That day had blown in and then blown out taking half the nearby area homes along with it, severely damaging the remainder. Now it was a memory, a thing the newspaper mentioned yearly, a bad thing that many remembered when the bland, smiling big-city weathermen on the television news mentioned tornado watches or warnings.

I parked the Toyota in Twiggens's side lot. Somewhere on campus I heard a bell toll the hour. It was now ten o'clock and I'd promised Jo I'd try hard to be home by ten-thirty.

The lot was dimly lighted and almost full. I checked it over, but found no orange VW (or my old Ford).

I walked in the front door. The bar started inside the door and ran in a semicircle. It wasn't a very large place but there were many booths in the darkness beyond the bar. A large, lone man worked behind the bar filling orders for handsome and lightly clad waitresses. The booths behind the bar were high-backed. No music played. For a time Dwight Wiggens, the owner and resident bartender, had curtained those individual booths, but I'd heard that someone from the local Alcoholic Beverage Board had complained and so the curtains were now gone. In recompense Wiggens had turned off more lights.

I'd known Dwight Wiggens for a while. He was an opportunistic man who'd once made part of his living as a small-time professional wrestler. When age had made him give that up and want to get away from the rest of his work as a welder in construction, he'd seen a need in Bington and shrewdly filled it.

It was widely reported that there were several bars in Bington for area male homosexuals, but until Dwight opened Twiggens, none for the females. Now, as Bington grew and progressed, there was one.

Dwight nodded at me from behind his bar. I took a stool. The bar itself was vacant, but the booths behind teemed with life. Waitresses made speed runs delivering drinks and I could hear the soft sound of female voices now that I was seated, low voices, whispers.

It was too late for dinner, but I'd heard from someone that Dwight Wiggens had a first-class kitchen.

Dwight and I smiled at each other.

"I ain't dead sure, but I don't think this is your kind of place, Robak," he ventured, grinning.

We'd not always been friendly, but these days we were congenial. When he'd first tried to open the bar I'd appeared at a zoning meeting to represent neighbors, mostly professorial types, who'd objected. They'd not objected to the lesbian part because they'd not known of it then. They'd just not wanted a zoning change and a bar so near the storm-damaged houses that remained.

They'd wanted the area to remain residential, no Convenient Stores, no Arby's, and no damned bars.

My clients and I had kept Dwight from getting that zoning change the first year. He'd not liked that even though I'd been polite and reasonable in my presentation at my clients' request. Still, I'd watched him getting madder and madder.

He'd gone public in his dislike in front of city hall after the zoning meeting. He'd come at me, long arms extended, trying for a wrestler's hold, wanting to hurt me, his face both angry and frustrated.

I'd hit him a few times when he'd rushed me, a few more when I'd stepped aside and he'd run past me, and two good ones as he was turning. I hadn't hurt him much. He was built like a tank. People stepped between us. A police car stopped across the street.

I'd been glad.

Later, after a change in city administration and a granting of the zoning change, I'd stopped by his newly opened place and bought him a congratulatory drink. I'd not appeared in his second hearing. My old clients had again objected to the bar, but this time they'd hired a new lawyer, someone who was less of a hooligan than I was, someone who didn't brawl in public places.

Then, later than that, I'd gone past the funeral home when Dwight's wife had died of cancer. The funeral parlor had been almost deserted and not many names were on the visitation book. I'd written mine there and stayed with him until visitation was over. I liked him. He liked me.

Dwight leaned across the bar and shook my hand, continuing. "Unless you've had a sex change that I ain't heard about, this ain't your style." He nodded, appraising me. "Try three blocks over and two down. Chas-

by's. It's for boys." He looked back at his booths anx-
iously. My coming seemed to have stirred a little extra
sound back there.

I patted the back of his hand suggestively and made
him grin some more.

"I need a scotch and water. Make sure there's no lipstick on the glass," I said in a low voice.

He mixed me a quickie while I looked him over. He
had cauliflower ears and a nose that bent three ways,
but he wasn't a bad guy. He was high fiftyish and
maybe two-sixty at an inch or two less than six feet, and
he was usually easygoing until some bastard lawyer
riled him.

"I got a note for you behind the bar," he said matter-
of-factly. "I don't know why any of my nice ladies
would write you or would expect you to even come in
here, but someone did."

I'd heard around that Dwight ran a maildrop for his
customers. Ladies wrote other ladies about whatever it
was that interested them and Dwight put the notes,
many of them anonymous, in a box behind his bar and
delivered them to the addressee.

I wasn't totally surprised that there was a note for
me.

I took what he gave me. It was a single piece of yellow
lined paper, like the one Steinmetz had given me in the
hospital. It was folded over and my name was on the
outside. I opened it.

The note was printed in block letters. It read: "Last
warning. Don't look no more. Leave us alone. Please."
There was no signature.

"Do you remember who gave you this?" I asked
Dwight.

He shook his head. "They stick them in boxes on the

booth tables. This one came from one of the boxes. Lots
of times they'll put 'em in a box where no one has been
sitting. This one was like that." He left me for a moment and made drinks for a waitress. I put some money
on the bar to cover my drink and I had a sip of it. Infe-
rior bar scotch, but expensive in here. Dwight showed
them no mercy on prices.

He returned. "Hoo hoo, boy. You got 'em all shook up
back in boothland. The barmaid said a couple of the
ladies had asked who you were and now they know because she done told. So some of them are worried. Some
of them back there are married and still working at it."

"I'll leave in a moment, Dwight. Things will then
settle back down. I'm looking for some youngish ladies
from out of town. One of them would be black and built
very strong. Another might act sick. There may be a
third lady. All I know about her is she's been described
as 'pretty.' "

"They come and go, Don," he said. "I stay out of
their business. They don't like me messing in it. I got
some black ladies who come in. I get lots of pretties. I
get sickies also. I get professors' wives and politicians'
girlfriends. I get ladies who come in here who'd raise
your eyebrows high if you saw their faces. I ain't noticed no group like you describe, but then I try to pay as
little attention as possible. I do my bar biz and leave
their biz to them." He shook his head mournfully, cauliflower ears outlined by the small neon light of a
Budweiser beer sign in his front window. "I mean these
kind of ladies get angry when one of us men gets out in
the circle of things."

"I hope you're making lots of money," I said.

He nodded. "I'm doin' jus' fine."

One of the waitresses, the prettiest one I'd seen, came

to where we were. She tapped on the bar. "A lady back there wants a whiskey sour, a plain tonic water, and a scotch on the rocks." She looked over at me, not really seeing me at all. "And him out of here."

Dwight nodded. "By, Don."

I was home by ten-thirty, much to Jo's surprise and delight.

Contacting Doctor Hugo S. Buckner on a Sunday morning would seem like hard business, but it wasn't. On Sunday doctors' offices are closed and doctors' answering services are vague. On Sunday hospital routines relax, some doctors go to church, and the whole day can get screwed up for the unhealthy if they have a seizure or a snakebite or an infected hangnail.

But I owned inside information. I *knew* where Doc Buckner almost always ate his Sunday breakfast.

I drove the Toyota downtown and found the one I wanted of the three or four Bington establishments that opened on Sunday morning to take care of the late night drunk and wifeless crowd. I walked inside and located Doc in a back booth, eating link sausages and eggs and jellied rye toast and drinking from an oversized coffee cup. A waitress hovered close by and two locals sat across from Doc pumping free advice out of him.

The cook stood by the kitchen door listening respectfully. The cook knew me so I got a negligent wave of the hand.

I sat down next to Buckner and waited my turn. The waitress brought me a cup of coffee and I drank it with care. It was very hot and strong, black and bitter enough to kill an Ohio River catfish.

Buckner answered another question or two and then deigned to notice me.

"How about Steinmetz, Doc?" I asked. "I need to get in and ask him some questions. It's getting to be urgent."

He shook his head. "Not on your life or his, Robak. Right now he and I do our communicating through eye-winks and we do damn little of that. I think he can talk and will soon talk, but he's not strong yet. He could die today, he could die tomorrow. He could also live on for years."

"He could die in several ways," I said. I leaned close to him so that the others around couldn't hear. "Someone's after his money. Someone may have stolen his will, if he had one. Someone has been in his house. And that someone may try to kill him."

Doc looked apologetic. He cut a half-link bite of sausage and smeared it in egg yolk. "Can't help it or you, Robak. There's a new policeman three times a day, eight-hour shifts. George Gentrup sent them to keep watch outside Steinmetz's hospital room door, and no one goes in and out other than me and the special duty nurses. And no one gets to be a special duty nurse unless I know them and have known them ten years. So Steinmetz is safe." He thought on that for a moment as he chewed. "He gets a little better, he lasts another few days, and maybe I'll let you in to see him for a little while, but not now. And I want you to know, if he comes back to your office to work I'm not optimistic about his chances over the long run."

"You think office work would kill him?"

"The tension could." He shook his head. "The booze he'd drink and you and Jake would buy for him could."

"He'll drink no matter what you say or what we say."

"That's true. He is a stubborn old bastard." He looked at his watch. "I'm going to go check him again in a few minutes."

"To the hospital?"

He nodded placidly.

"On a Sunday?"

"Contrary to what you seem to think I go there almost every Sunday." He smiled. "I'm not a lawyer. I'm a healer, a doctor of medicine. Our courthouses of the sick don't close because it's Sunday, Christmas, Memorial Day, or St. Swithin's Birthday."

The cook nodded positively from the doorway. "Way to tell him, Doc."

I eyed the cook. "Go die of cholesterol poisoning or something."

He grinned.

"I'm working today," I said, ignoring the cook again and addressing Doc Buckner. "Could I just follow you to the hospital and look in the window?"

"No. You'd surely excite him. He'd start thinking about Early Times like a five-year-old thinks of Christmas." He held up a hand. "Joking aside, Don, I can't let you see him at all. Not yet."

"Will you get in touch with me as soon as you can?"

"Sure."

"Okay. And will you tell Steinmetz we're all thinking about him and that we said hello."

"Yes. I'll do that. Did your office people tell you I wanted to see you?"

"They did. I hoped it was about Steinmetz."

"No, not Steinmetz. Stanley Willetts's mother came to my office. She's been a patient of mine for years. She's a tiny little lady who weighs about ninety pounds. Feisty and mean. She made me promise to tell you that her Stanley's a good man and that he wouldn't bludgeon his tramp wife to death even if she did need it really bad."

"That's interesting. It's just the kind of evidence I need to get Sheriff Goldie and Herman Leaks to release Stanley on his own recognizance. I'll go and tell Goldie that Stan didn't kill his wife because Stan's mother says so. Stanley will then get released." I nodded. "The law works that way, Doc."

Doc placidly chewed some more sausage. "Well, she just wanted me to say that to you and make sure you knew that Stanley's wife was running around on him."

"Does she know who the person was that the wife was running with?"

"She didn't mention any names. I knew Stanley's wife. She was handsome and had the reputation of being available. Especially with Stanley away on so many forced vacations."

"Did you do the autopsy on her?"

"I examined the corpse. The cause of death was apparent. Someone stove her head in, again and again. They kept doing it long after she was dead."

"Yeah. Like a jealous husband. Tell Stan's mother you talked to me. Tell her I'm doing all I can." I got up from the booth. *But I wasn't doing anything or at least I wasn't yet.*

I turned back to Doc. "Had she had sex any time close to her time of death?"

"Nope. No sex. Just hammer marks."

I went back to the truck and got in and sat behind the wheel. I riffled through Stanley's file. The copy of the printout of Stanley's record drew my eye once more. The list was long. Burglary, conversion, theft, shoplifting. Pages of offenses.

And not one of the crimes was violent. That could be because Stanley had always been the thief until someone stole his usually wayward wife instead of just borrowing her overnight or weekly while Stanley was in jail.

The house that had belonged to the now deceased Ruby Geneva (Honey) Willetts sat on a small lot in the village of Dublin, three miles from Bington. Dublin was as old as Bington, but it had only four hundred people. The village sat away from the water on the far side of a state highway. High hills bounded the nonriver side. The river side of the road had new construction, boat docks, and a small motel. Some of the houses in and around Dublin had been bought by the tourist trade and by oldsters looking for a cheap place to retire, a place to laze away the days and sleep soundly at night.

Honey's house was old and looked ramshackle, but up close it seemed sound. It sat in the north hill part of the village, farthest from the river, and therefore probably not as desirable as those in the south part of the village. Her house was surrounded by others almost like it, some of them in disrepair, some, like Honey's, not that bad. The lane in front of the house was gravel and cinder. It was narrow and ended fifty yards north in a turnaround on the side of a hill.

Sheriff Goldie or his people had put a yellow "Police Line" banner across the front of the door, but Goldie had also furnished me the house key when I requested it. I unlocked the door and bent to step under the yellow band. I could see someone watching me from the porch shadows of the house to the north of Honey's. I waved that way and ducked inside.

The front room was a living room. I tried a switch
and a hanging ceiling light came on. The room was
brightly papered and attractive. There was a decent
couch with a coffee table in front of it. There was a
lounge chair and a walnut-stained stand with a television set. I flipped it on and a brightly robed television
preacher exhorted me for funds to carry on his true
work. The TV picture was good. I turned the television
off and looked around some more. There were pictures
on the walls that looked as if they'd been bought from
starving artists. One was a sympathetic Jesus, hands
outstretched, the other a huge-eyed deer in a forest. I
opened a drawer in the coffee table, but there was nothing inside.

The next room back was a dining room. Matched
chairs surrounded a well-polished table. A cupboard
held some china and a few pieces of cheap silver plate.
From one wall a pilgrim looked down and from another
the sea broke wildly against a cold beach. Starving artists again. The kitchen behind had a window on one
side. The cupboards were crowded with big, commer-
cial-sized cans of canned goods and the refrigerator had
frozen steaks in the freezer part and a minor amount of
souring food in the cool side. There was a medium
good, new-looking electric stove, plus a microwave. I
checked the shelves and drawers for anything of interest.

Nothing.

Behind the kitchen was a bedroom and bath. The bed
in the bedroom was king-size. It was covered with a
bright yellow spread and the yellow was spotted with
dried blood. Someone had drawn in chalk the outline of
a human figure in the rug on the floor beside the bed. I
stayed away from that spot. There was no closet, but

there was a chest of drawers and a bureau. Clothes lay
folded neatly. It looked like all of them were Honey's. If
Stanley had ever lived in this house there was now no
trace of it in what remained.

In the chest of drawers I did find a few letters from
Stanley in prison. They were not of interest. There was
also a book of photographs. An envelope of photos yet
to be mounted was in the rear of the album.

I read the letters carefully. There were no threats in
them, no hints that Stanley was angry. I wondered if
someone had other letters with threats in them. If so,
Prosecutor Herman hadn't furnished them to me yet. I
went through the photo album. Most of the snapshots
in it had to be Honey. She was a woman with a pleasant, vacuous face; not beautiful, but handsomely put together, sturdy and yet curved. In some of the early
pages in the album Stanley stood beside her. Two were
taken in what appeared to be either a work camp or a
prison. Honey and Stanley held hands across a picnic
table. There was a high fence and a guard tower behind
them.

At the back of the album most of the photos were of
Honey alone. Honey working in her garden, Honey,
muscular legs up on her couch, watching television.
Honey standing, Honey smiling. Maybe self-taken. Set
a timer dial on the camera and then hurry to your pose.
Ten seconds and say "cheese."

At the back of the book there were more openings for
photos, the openings still vacant. I was unsure whether
any of those openings had ever been occupied.

Some early photos were of what I believed to be family, Honey's family, plus maybe some friends or neighbors. In one Honey stood with an older woman, arm in
arm. I recognized the other woman as Honey's mother,

Mildred. The picture looked as if it had been taken some years back. There was also one of Honey, same time period, with a thin, small woman. Both stood stiffly, both wore forced smiles. I thought that this older lady beside Honey might be Stanley's mother. A family get-together with maybe wife and mother-in-law knowing that something was going on outside the marriage. Not comfortable.

I found nothing of real interest and nothing that helped explain, assuming Stanley hadn't done it, why a shadowy someone had used a sledge hammer and smashed in the pleasant face of Honey Willetts again and again in her bedroom.

The photo album was like a sterile room in a hospital.

Maybe someone had stayed, after Honey was dead, and tidied up the house, taking away all that would mean anything to someone like me or Goldie or the state police technicians. I looked again at the back of the album and the gaps in the later pages.

And maybe Honey herself had cleaned her past life by removing most of Stanley. What was left were prim pictures, no kisses, no hugs, just hands held with a backdrop of prison.

I sat down on a corner chair and thought about it, trying to make it come clear. What the sheriff and the prosecutor believed seemed likely. The woman in the photos had never waited faithfully before for a husband in prison. But this time maybe she'd found someone (or several someones), who'd given her money, bought her household furnishings and food. Or maybe her mother had helped, although that didn't sound much like Mildred Standish. This time Honey was prepared to abandon Stanley. Then he'd appeared on her doorstep, seen

the new television set, the microwave, the good furniture. Seen that there had to be someone else.

He'd first raged and, later, killed.

Logical enough. Why didn't I believe it?

I took one picture of Honey out of the album. I put it
in my pocket and put the album back away.

The bathroom had the usual bathroom stuff. There
was a tub with shower, antiseptically clean. There was a
medicine cabinet and a large, lighted mirror above and a
washbowl that still held a few hairs near the drain. I
opened the medicine cabinet and found Bufferin, first
aid stuff, lipsticks and powder, some prescription medicine. I examined the boxes and envelopes. There were
things for allergies, colds, pain, and fevers. There was
an almost empty vial of birth control pills that had been
last filled a few months back. Three pills left. There was
a small tinfoil folder that I curiously opened. A tiny bit
of white powder remained in the folder. I thought it
might be cocaine, but I was unsure. If Goldie had not
found it I'd tell him of it, but my guess was he had and
ignored it. Cocaine and pot are everywhere in college
towns.

I gave the bathroom up and went back to the bedroom. I poked under each layer of clothes. Honey favored skirts and sweaters and frilly panties. I removed
drawers and looked behind them and under them.

Nothing. I found no camera, but thought that maybe
a relative or friend had already latched onto it and ap-
propriated it. *Something of value. Take it before someone else
gets it.*

I walked slowly to the front of the house. Without
Honey the place was as empty as a football field after
the game.

Nothing.

I tried to make an assessment of the woman who'd once lived in the house. Stanley had not said where she worked or all of what she'd done, but he had said she'd worked, "part-time," as a fill-in waitress around the university. He'd not mentioned family money, but what I knew indicated to me that there was little, other than what I'd heard about the lottery dollars, if that was true. Somehow Honey had survived and prospered. Maybe her mother Mildred could tell me how? In Bington there was no easy way to make money even if Honey had gone professional. There was a horde of amateur competition frolicking in the local bars in ages that ranged from adventurous high school girls on up to desperate senior citizens.

I opened the front door and went back under the yellow banner carefully. I shut and locked the door behind me. I walked off the porch and into the front yard.

The person who'd watched me from the house north of Honey's stood in her own front yard. She was an older lady, medium in size, dressed in clothes too heavy for the weather. She shivered in the small, warm wind and beckoned to me.

"Hey now," she called. "You come on over here."

I nodded and took one more look at the exterior of Honey's house. It needed paint. Honey had seen that also. Someone, and I thought it was Stanley, had started scraping the peeling paint off the housefront.

There was no fence and so I walked from yard to yard.

"You're that lawyer, ain't you? I seen your picture in the paper before," the old lady said. Her face was a round map composed of wrinkles. Somewhere in the wrinkles there were small islands that were her features. Her lips were almost lost in the wrinkled sea, but

her eyes were still bird-bright and interested in the
world around her. She looked me over.

"My name's Robak," I said. "And I'm a lawyer. I was
appointed by Judge Harner to represent Stanley Willetts."

She nodded approvingly. "I'm Mrs. Chastain, Maude
Chastain. I've lived here next to Honey ever since she
bought her house, maybe ten years now. We neighbored
a little. She liked to keep mostly to herself. Funny-actin'
little lady. Night person. Sleep most of the day, every
day."

"Did someone move in with her while Stanley was in
jail this last time?"

"Maybe so, maybe no. Now and again someone
would come to the house late. She liked to party. I'd
wake up in the night and see a nice car parked over
there. But come mornin' and it'd be gone. Lots of times
a car would pull up and drop Honey off late. I'd hear
laughin' and talkin' then. What she was doin' she was
mostly doin' somewhere else I'd reckon."

"What kind of car?"

She shook her head, unsure. "Various."

"How about work?"

"She worked some, waitressed now and then around
town or at the university. She did some baby-sitting.
Lately she wasn't doing much of either. Except sleepin'
durin' the day and givin' Stanley orders after they let
him out of prison again."

"I looked in her refrigerator and cabinets. She ate
well."

The bird eyes gave me a quick glance. "I'd not know
about that," she said primly. "I loaned her a cup of
sugar once. One time I borrowed two eggs from her and
had to wake her up by beating on the door. I never took

supper with her and never offered it. I was in her house
maybe twice. She had some nice things, prints and real
silver and the like."

"Nothing like that there now," I said.

She shrugged. "Relatives and friends maybe."

"Did you hear anything at all the night she was
killed?"

"Ah, now we're to it. I heard her mister cussing her
out in the late afternoon. I heard her order him off and
say she was going to call the law if he stayed one minute
longer. She came to the window and I heard and saw
her tell him that. She was in her pajamas and it was a
long way from dark. She liked to wear shortie see-
throughs from them dirty stores you can find in the
malls in Louisville. Maybe he left and come back later. I
didn't see or hear nothin' if he did. Not of him."

"Then you heard nothing after he left?"

She reached down. She stood near a flowering bush.
She caressed a flower with a withered hand. It seemed
to steady her. "I didn't say that."

"Can you tell me what you heard?"

"It wasn't much. Mildred came to the door in the
early evening."

"Honey's mother?"

"Yeah. Mildred Standish. I'd not seen much of her at
the house for months, not while Stanley was in prison.
But she was there that night and then she left. I could
hear them talking, but I couldn't make out what was
said. It sounded friendly enough."

"Anything else?"

"Later there were some sounds came from over there
about the time the paper said Honey died. Nighttime.
Her time to be awake. I told the sheriff about it, but it
didn't seem to much impress him."

"Did you see or hear a car at Honey's house that night?"

"No, not after Mildred left in her old clunker. There could have been one a bit down the road, where you'll have to go to turn when you leave. I seen someone walk through the yard to the road carryin' somethin' late that night."

I waited, knowing there was more.

"Nothin' big. Maybe a box of stuff. It was right dark. The box seemed heavy and whoever it was made two trips." She nodded to herself. "I told Goldie about it. He said it was likely her jailbird husband taking somethin' along with him to eat or drink after he killed Honey."

Something came to me.

"Man or woman?"

"I guess a man. I didn't think it was Stanley, but it could have been. I don't see that good these days. Cataracts."

"How about you, Mrs. Chastain. Do you work somewhere?"

"Social security," she said. "Uncle Sam plus a check from welfare. Welfare's took 'em a lien on my house. They'll get it one day when I'm gone." She smiled up at me. "Did I help any?"

"Maybe." I got out my billfold and found a twenty in it and gave it to her. "I'd like for you to keep a watch on Honey's house in case anyone should come snooping. Just watch and don't do anything else. Write down what you see."

She took the twenty and folded it and put it into a pocket. Her hands trembled a little, but the shivering had stopped. "Sure. You bet."

EIGHT

"Steinmetz's Memoirs" (manuscript) page 145: "Is it possible for parents and their children to hate each other? Of course it is. It's easy."

ON MONDAY MORNING, despite the fact that I had other things that needed early starts, I ran. I was behind on my running schedule and not running had made me irritable. So, at the request of both of my immediate family members, I ran.

I ran along the river. I had on my best set of running shorts and a new t-shirt without anything on it, plain white, no pictures, no words. I figured if I died during the run at least I'd not be mistaken as a student or a professor at the state university. I wore my almost new Rockports. I left the Toyota parked in a public lot along the river in the center of town.

I ran at my usual pace, not fast, not slow. I wasn't a record seeker or a marathoner. I was running to stay in shape.

It was hot. The river ran high and was still mud brown. The sun was in my face. It looked as if it was going to be another year where the Ohio Valley spring would be only a pause between winter and summer.

Some days other people joined me when I ran. On many days the river path was thick with them, either running with me, or near me. On this day, with it being hot, humid, and Monday, I ran alone. People hate Mondays. I hate Mondays.

I saw other people along the river. Boaters launched boats and fishermen rowed past. Now and then someone I knew would call out to me and I'd raise an arm in greeting to them and keep on running. You can't visit and run at the same time.

There was a walking/running path and I used it. The weeds, from the rain and heat, had already grown high on each side of it. But, because of the river and its rise and fall, there were few trees and bushes where the river had risen during the spring floods. The river had washed the new growth away and eaten away at the few survivors.

Perhaps to punish myself for missing earlier days I ran until it hurt some and until I strained for breath. I ran until the only recognizable smell that came through to me was the fish odor of the river, overpowering the other odors of late spring.

Then I slowed. I became aware again of more than the path I ran on.

I suddenly had the feeling that someone was watching me. Once, long before, I'd been in a war, and some things from it had never left me. People had tried their best to kill me then. Others had tried since then. And therefore, I was sensitive to eyes on me, aware of them. I ran on and began to look around me.

All I saw at first was the traffic on the river road above me. It seemed to be normal morning traffic. People drove along the town river road, Front Street. People drove it before going to work as a part of their daily routine. On some days you could see the Delta Queen or the Mississippi Queen passing or tied to the bank. A short wait would almost always bring a towboat past hauling something up or down river. And so residents and tourists drove the road, enjoying it, soothed by both its changes and sameness.

I kept seeing one car again and again. It was an older Plymouth, indeterminate in color, dark and dusty, maybe deep beige or grey. It would stay at about my running speed, then get ahead, then pull into one of the viewing areas that bordered Front Street. Out and then in and then out again.

We drew near the east edge of town and I saw the Plymouth waiting above me in the last viewing lot. Someone rolled down the driver's window and waved a handkerchief in the breeze. I wondered if they were waving to me. I decided not to wave back, but to ignore the gesture.

Sometimes I ran on past the edge of town. Past the city limit the path was more rugged and there were fewer houses. Not many people ran that far or used that continuing path.

I decided against it for today. I didn't like the car above me or the wave of the handkerchief. Maybe someone waited further on. There were a dozen places past the city limits where someone could lie in wait for me.

I turned back and ran the other direction, back to the center of things.

If the occupant of the old Plymouth cared, I saw nothing from that car after the brief wave of a handkerchief. Maybe it was only a friendly wave to me, Robak the runner.

I didn't see the old Plymouth again.

I ran past where I'd parked the Toyota and on toward the west part of town. After a while I'd had enough and so I turned back and ran to where I'd parked the truck.

I got inside, started the motor, and drove home without incident. I showered, shaved, and had my small breakfast with Jo and Joe, juice, toast, and coffee.

Joe was into oatmeal and raisin toast and lots of juice. He'd lost his baby fat look and now he was thin and wiry. I checked the papers, saw the Reds would be in town for the weekend, and made a call.

I told Joe and Jo that we had tickets to go see the Reds play Saint Louis and got kisses as a reward. The kisses were more nourishing than the rest of my breakfast.

I knew where Dwight Wiggens lived. At a little after eight I parked in his drive. The house was large and expensive-looking. An almost new Cadillac and a shiny 300Z sat in the open garage.

Wiggens was working in his yard when I stopped the car. He was employing one of those weed things you can buy from call-in television eight-hundred numbers, to grub between his flowers. I got out of the Toyota and walked toward him and he stopped his work.

"Got just a moment?" I asked.

He nodded easily. He was the kind of man who, once he'd decided he was for you, stayed that way. He'd made up his mind about me on the night we'd left the zoning meeting. I had, he believed, courage. I wasn't that sure. Sometimes I thought all I really owned was a nasty curiosity.

"Come up on the porch. It's already hot enough in the sun to boil up some soup." He walked up onto his shady porch and found a towel on a rocking chair there. He toweled off, exhibiting massive arms that hadn't deteriorated much since he'd been in the wrestling business.

I sat down in a chair he indicated and he took the

nearby swing. I could smell him and he smelled of old late-night booze and new-morning bay rum.

"You caused a stir among my sweet ladies Saturday night," he said, grinning about it. "Them nice ladies don't like having you around. The story I heard is that you're messing in something they don't want you messing in, looking for someone they don't want you to find. I guess that'd be Steinmetz's daughter. Saturday night, after you left, the place buzzed about it. My ladies stayed late and drank heavy. Good for one night business. But don't come again just now, Don. You being there and at the bar and us being friends makes them distrustful of me and that would, in the long run, be bad for biz. You need to know something, then come here or call me here at home before I leave for the bar. That's about eleven every day but Sunday."

"All right," I said. "I'll do it that way. I handed him Honey's picture. "How about this lady? Have you ever seen her before?"

He looked at it intently. "I've never seen her in my bar, but I know who she is. I read the local paper and listen to the radio."

"I thought maybe she might have been in—might even have worked for you there at the bar one time or another. She waitressed some."

He looked at the picture again. "She's never worked for me. That's certain. Now and then someone will call in sick and we've got some girls who work extra for us when that happens, but this lady ain't one of them." He shook his head. "She may have been in as a customer and I could have missed her." He smiled. "But I doubt it."

"I don't think you miss much, Dwight."

"I try not," he said, grinning. "I've got me a code. I

never say nothin' about what lady goes off with what other lady." He picked up the morning paper from the porch floor and fanned himself. "But it wouldn't stop me from tellin' you that I'd seen someone in the place." He handed me back the picture. "This one I've not seen. Now there's one more thing. There's this back entrance that the ladies can come through. Your lady could be inside every night and me not see her. The waitresses would, but I don't go back into the booth area unless there's trouble. Used to be there was more trouble than we have now. Some of them, early on, was like worms, but now it's monogamy and true love preached. And I do mean preached. This AIDS stuff got them scared, Don. I think that's the most of the reason they ain't so much switching around."

"Thanks for the info, Dwight. The lady in the picture is Honey Willetts, as you probably know from the papers and radio. Her husband Stanley's in jail for doing her in with a lot of whacks from a sledge hammer. They say he got out of prison and came home and then killed Honey. Maybe, if she was running with one or more of your ladies, he wasn't the jealous lover who did the job on her."

"I said I'd seen her before and I also read and heard about her getting killed," he said. "But I promise you I know nothin' that'll help you, Don. Murder makes me sick to my stomach. I had enough of blood. I had enough of hurt and dyin'. That's why I quit wrestlin'. Some of it's show, but the cheap purse stuff ain't. I couldn't take the real part anymore. Some guys fight real bad and I kept getting stuck in with them."

"Sounds like an interesting kind of job," I said.

"The show-off part is where the money's at. The fake stuff. If you're good enough you can make it big out

there. I got too old. No one identified with me. I didn't
make a bad enough villain and I didn't make a good
enough hero." He looked me over. "You're decent-look-
ing—make a good hero type. Put on twenty pounds and
I'll get you a try. You'd make money, maybe a lot more
than you make lawyering. I know all the tricks and I got
contacts."

I looked back at him and didn't smile. "Thanks. It's a
thought, Dwight. I got a pot I'd need to get rid of first.
Then I might take you up on it."

I wanted to go to jail to see Stanley Willetts, but I
decided I'd be received better if I went first to see Mildred Standish. Willetts wasn't going anyplace. He'd
keep.

Mildred Standish lived in one of Bington's oldest
homes, a barn of a place that was feeling its age badly.
Just looking at the old house was enough to ruin your
day. It needed a new roof, painting and pointing, new
gutters and downspouts, and someone to cut the yard
and trim the bushes. The house was on Main Street, six
blocks from Steinmetz's house.

Mildred was the widow of Ethan Standish, a hale fellow who'd been a Bington police officer and an off-duty
drunk for twenty plus years prior to his retirement.
He'd died soon after that retirement. I'd heard wags
about town tell that he'd died of a combination of ear
and liver failure and that Mildred had aided in his de-
mise by half talking him to death.

While Ethan had been alive I remembered better
things about the Main Street house. I recalled flowers,
paint, and close-cut grass. Now the house had gone
from neat and handsome to falling down and seedy.

I walked through weeds to the stone porch. The bell
ring was one of the old type and I had to twist it to
make it sound dimly inside.

It was now close on nine in the morning. The woman
who opened the door a few inches was still dressed in
her nightgown and had covered it with a careless robe.
She was late fiftyish and had gone to seed as badly as her
house. She sagged all over. I'd heard she was a drinker.
Maybe she'd learned that from her deceased husband.

She knew me and she nodded out of the crack in the
door.

"What do you want, Robak?"

"I got appointed for Stanley Willetts. I want to talk to
you about what he's accused of doing to his wife, your
daughter."

"Want away. I won't talk to you. You're representing
the wrong person to come on my property. Not only
that but you belong to the wrong party. I ain't about to
accommodate you."

I shrugged. "No skin off my nose. I think he did it
also, but until I talk to you and some others I'm not
going to plead him and get it over. And I think the
prosecutor will go along with me and force you to answer my questions."

"Herman's a wimp and you're a worser one, Robak,"
she said.

I waited. The door was still open.

"I guess, if I don't talk to you, I'll wind up in one of
Herman's anterooms getting deposed?" she asked.

"That's correct."

She thought on it for a long moment. "All right. You
can come in. We'll sit out on the back porch. I'll let you
have a cup of coffee, but nothing else. I don't break
bread with people from your party." She favored me

with an ugly smile full of manufactured menace. "I break bones."

"I know how tough you are, Mildred."

I followed behind her back through a dirty kitchen. Yesterday's dishes lay fallow in a chipped sink. She opened a bread box and dug out something wrapped in foil. She cut herself a piece of it and I saw it was some kind of breakfast roll. She put the cut piece into a microwave and she poured two cups of coffee. She put one on a tray and added something from a plain bottle to the other. The microwave beeped and she put the results on the tray and I followed her to the back porch. She handed me my coffee and I sat in the chair she indicated.

"Maybe you ain't as bad as Herman," she said reasonably, after a sip of her coffee etc. "Nobody could be that bad."

"How come you don't get along with Herm?" I asked.

She gave me a disgusted look. "No answers for you on that. Ask your questions."

"Tell me about your daughter."

"She got hammered to death by her jailbird husband. Your people run the state now, Robak. They shouldn't have let him loose, but they did. He sweet-talked them and, like the crappy, no-backbone group they are, they rolled over and played dead dogs for him. So he came back and hammered my daughter."

"I got told you wanted your daughter to divorce him?"

"You bet I did. There have been lots of men around she could have had, but all she wound up doing with her life was waiting for simple Stanley to get out of jail. A waste."

"Faithfully waiting?"

Mildred smiled.

"Who'd she been going with while he was in prison this last time?"

"I don't know."

"Come on, Mildred. You'd know."

She shook her head. "I wasn't that close with her. She got to be sixteen and she informed me and Ethan that she knew what was good for her and that we was to butt completely out. She moved out. I had the probation people bring her back a couple of times, but she'd just move out again. Ethan and I talked and let her go. From that time on she ran her life."

"Did you visit her?"

"Not much. A couple of months ago I ran into her on the street and I offered to come up with the money for her to get a lawyer and divorce Stanley. I told her I'd pay for it at the court clerk's door, knowing that if I just gave her money, she'd blow it on something else. After that, now and then, she'd call me and we'd talk and I'd renew the offer. But she never said who she was going with and I didn't ask."

"I heard you won some lottery money and you gave some of that to her."

"I gave it all to her. I had my reasons for doing it."

"What are they?"

"None of your affair."

I adopted a new tack. "Could someone have killed her who maybe she'd gone with at some earlier time?"

"Anything's possible, but I'm betting on Stanley. I guess I'd have maybe known if there was someone else close because I hear lots, but no one hears it all." She looked morosely out into the bright morning.

I had a sudden empathy of the moment with her. She'd spent her life as a drunken policeman's wife and widow. She'd lost her only daughter as a family member early. She'd gotten herself into low-level and then high-profile party work because, I believed, it was something to do and gave her a cause to work for. Now her husband and daughter were dead and, even if she was capable of loving them only a little, they were the most of what she'd had. So now she had one love left, her political party. She had one big hate, Stanley. She had a hundred, hundred smaller hates. I was one of them. *But I wondered about the lottery money.*

"Someone did kill your daughter, Mildred. Stanley swears he's not the one. Think about it. He's always been an easy out in the game before. He'd do a job, get caught, plead, and do his time. Your prosecutor isn't after him for big stuff like the death penalty or a ton of years. But this time Stanley is saying no. He's saying he didn't do it. I talked to him in jail. I thought he was angry and confused and sad about Honey's death."

"Don't you call her Honey," she said. "Her name was Ruby Geneva Standish. I hated that nickname. She picked it out for herself. No one named her that."

"All right. But think about Stanley and whether he's the one. He's spent a lifetime doing piddling, little crimes. He's never hurt anyone. He's stolen a thousand things and burglarized a hundred stores. He's a thief, but is he a killer?"

She looked down at the dirty back porch floor. A tiny breeze blew over us. "I don't know, Robak. He's your job of work. I've thought some on some of the things you're saying, but I still get back to thinking that maybe he just got mad and killed her. He's a worthless bastard. She called me and I was out to her house in the evening of the night she died. I thought she was about to make up her mind to go ahead and divorce him. She'd used up the money I gave her on her house and so I offered her the divorce money again, but then she said she was still thinking on it. She told me she had Stanley working on her house and that she was thinking that maybe, if he'd promise to go to work and quit being a burglar, then she'd take him back." She took a sip from her cup. "She said she'd run him off for the day, but she knew he'd be back around pestering her the next."

I nodded and waited.

"She showed me inside her house. She was proud of the house. Nice things. Pretty paintings on the wall. Just like in rich people's houses where I've been."

"Someone paid for those nice things and those pretty paintings."

She nodded in agreement. "She used the money I gave her. No one was living there with her. I looked around when we walked through the house. There were things which would have told me, extra toothbrushes, shaving stuff, things hanging. But there was nothing. Maybe someone had lived there and she'd had them leave what with Stanley coming back home." She shook her head. "Clean as a pin."

"Lots of food in the refrigerator."

She frowned. "One of the deputies said that. She never had more than a couple of cans before."

"What do you think?"

"I don't know. It's your job. You look."

"I did. I was at the house. I went through it. I talked to a neighbor."

She gave me an approving look.

"Stanley thinks you're out to get him," I said.

"Let him think that. Maybe I am."

"Tell me about the lottery money?" I asked again.

She nodded. "Maybe you got a right to know. I won

some. I hit for five thousand. Lots of people think it was more. I gave it to her."

"Why would you do that?"

"I don't need the money any more."

"Come on. You could use it. This house is falling apart."

"No. It'll last plenty long enough. I got cancer, Robak. I'm terminal. I don't need nothing any more. Three to six months. That's what they said. Now go blat that around."

"I won't say anything."

She nodded. "I hope you don't. I want you to know if there was a way I could send Stan ahead of me I'd do it."

"But you don't know whether he killed her or not."

She looked out into her back yard some more. I looked also. I saw weeds. I wasn't sure what she saw. The sun had gone behind a cloud and it was cooler. She shivered and pulled her thin robe tight about her. "I get chilled real easy these days."

"Answer me something. Could your daughter have been involved in any kind of a lesbian relationship?"

She looked surprised and then she shook her head emphatically. "That's not possible."

I sipped my own coffee. I watched her as she thought some more on it.

"She didn't much like other women. She had a friend or two, someone she could call on when there was more than one man. She started being boy crazy when she was about thirteen. She got worse. She moved out because we were trying to restrict her dates. It was always men. No women."

"When you and she talked, what would you talk about other than a divorce?"

"Nothing special. She'd ask how I was and how I was doing. She'd tell me a little about what she was doing. Sometimes she waitressed. I thought she got back to me and wanted me in her life a little because maybe she was lonely. So then I gave her the five thousand dollars minus the tax they took out and she cried a little. She kissed me and she hadn't done that since she was thirteen or so. She called me a few days later and said she'd spent it all on her house. Caught the mortgage up and bought some nice things."

"Was that before Stanley came home?"

"A little while."

"Why wouldn't she tell him about it when he wanted to know where the new stuff had come from?"

"I don't know."

Mildred thought a little more and I saw her face change. "Maybe this lesbian thing is something you made up, Robak. It could be something to help Stanley get off if he's tried. Something dirty to show and tell a jury and let them snicker over. That'd be like you, Robak. I heard about you when you was in the legislature."

I shook my head. "It's a useless defense, Mildred. I only wondered if she'd ever done anything like that or you'd ever seen anything along that line. I'm not about to try a woman in court who got a sledge hammer used on her head. I'm not that stupid."

She eyed me uncertainly.

"Try to remember anything else you can. If something comes along that might help me then call me at the office."

"No, I won't call. You know it. I did have one good reason to ask you in this morning. I wanted to know about Judge Steinmetz."

"He's about the same. I'm hoping to be able to see him sometime soon."

"When you do, tell him I asked after him. He was the best we ever had." She smiled at me sardonically. "And all those bad things I said about you earlier?"

I waited.

"I take back half of them."

I shook hands with her at the door. "I'll tell Steinmetz you asked about him."

"Yeah," she said laconically. "Tell him I'm fine, just fine."

I went back to the Toyota and drove away. All the way down the street I could see her standing on the porch watching me.

NINE

"Steinmetz's Memoirs (manuscript) page 232: "In my opinion sheriffs are the best of police officers because they're the only ones who have to stand before the public for election. So a sheriff will think twice before he starts silliness."

SHERIFF GOLDIE had his feet propped up on his desk. He gnawed blissfully at an already well-chewed cigar.

"You need a match," I said.

"Smoking is bad for your health even if our area farmers do grow *mucho* tobacco," he said virtuously. "Your client's been asking for you."

"In a couple of minutes I'd like to go in and see him, but before that I'd like to ask you something," I said, remembering something George Gentrup had told me and which I'd forgotten until now.

He raised an eyebrow.

"George Gentrup mentioned you had something going on out in the county that you weren't telling him about."

Goldie smiled mysteriously. "The reason I ain't is he's sometimes over-nosy. Even nosier than you, Don. George's jurisdiction ends at the city limits, but he's always into my business." He waved a calm hand. "Now don't you get me wrong. George is a fine boy and a good police officer—like he's dedicated and brave and

smart and all that. If I had to go in someplace rough I'd
want him with me. But I don't like him wanting to
know what I find out every time I turn over a rock out
in the county. If I think he ought to know then I inform
him, but if I think it's my stuff then he don't know
about it until I go to the prosecutor with it. And this
time I ain't gone that far yet. And maybe I won't need
to go that direction and the federal boys will take up on
it. But I been thinking some, before you asked your
question just now, that I might tell you about it."

I stood in front of him and waited.

He shook his head uncertainly. "I swear it ain't got
nothing to do with Stanley, Don. You let me sit here
and think some more on it and figure on how I can tell
it while you go on back and see your client. There's lots
for me to think on. I ain't supposed to say a word. As
for your client, he's in the same cell he was. My deputies just took the Monday morning penitents to county
court, leaving me alone to hold down things. I got to
watch the phone and take care of the office here. You go
up alone and talk. Then come back down and maybe I'll
tell you some about what us industrious county officers
have turned up." He smiled at me and it changed his
face pleasantly. "You'll be the first outside the department to hear about it unless someone of my people has
already sneaked it elsewhere. And you get it only when
you promise me you'll keep your mouth plumb shut
until I get to the bottom of it. I mean unless you can
show me it's got something to do with something you're
working on now."

"Sure. That's easy."

Stanley Willetts lay in his bunk. He had an aging
Popular Science magazine turned toward the light and he

was reading, sounding out the long words aloud. He saw me and put down his magazine. He smiled a good smile and I was impressed. My being impressed was tempered with the remembrance that once I'd represented a serial killer who'd done in at least a dozen and maybe two dozen in his wanderings. He'd owned one of the finest smiles I'd ever seen off a Hollywood screen. My serial killer was into watching, then breaking and entering farm homes to rape and rob and pillage, killing the occupants so that there were no witnesses left to testify against him. Thereafter he liked to do interesting things with the bodies.

The smile had brought him a horde of admirers (unfortunately for him, none were on the jury) in the courtroom watching while the trial progressed. Women and men had tried to pass him mash notes. That had been one of the court-appointed cases I'd tried and lost, the kind of case where I'd wondered what I'd done that had kept the jury deliberating for more than an hour. Most juries are pretty good and can see straight through the things that lawyers, who are advocates for their side of a case, place before them, but sometimes . . . My client still wrote me from the prison where he was supposed to spend the rest of his life. I shuddered at the thought he might escape.

"I'm glad to see you," Stanley said.

"I've been working on your situation. I need to ask you a few more questions."

"Yes sir."

"When you were off in prison at times before, you said your wife ran around on you. Do you know who she ran with?"

"Various. She wasn't very selective. Maybe that's why she married me, although you hope against hope there's more to marrying than there is to just sex." He shook his head forlornly. "I checked on the old lovers this time out, Mr. Robak. It wasn't any of them. Two of them have moved on, one up and died, and one's real sick. That left two. I followed them around. They're both married, and both are still cheating on their old ladies, but not with Honey. I don't think there was anyone steady this time or they was being awful careful."

"Sure?"

"Pretty sure. I watched careful and I waited careful. I was afraid that Honey would catch me if I stayed close all the time to her house, so I watched other houses, their houses."

"How about women?"

"Women friends?"

"No. Sometimes women get involved with other women. I'm sure you've seen homosexuality in prison. Women do that also."

"Not Honey," he said confidently. "She liked men. The times I was gone she took up with men. She'd need one and she'd get one. It was always men."

"Did she have any good female friends?"

"Maybe some girls she worked with. When I was home we usually went out alone. We seldom called other folks. Just Honey and me. We'd go someplace and dance. She liked to dance and dream. Maybe we'd have a couple of beers. Most of the time we'd spend at home, me working on her house for her, painting, remodeling, fixing, her supervising the maintenance of her nest. She loved her house, Mr. Robak."

"Her house was her nest?"

"That's what she called it. When I had money I'd give it to her and she'd take it right to the building association and pay it on the house. She wanted it fixed so no one could ever take it from her. Her name only. I called the building association and asked, claiming I was with a finance company. The house is paid up to date."

"What else can you tell me about her that might help?"

He shook his head sadly. "She was lazy, Mr. Robak. She liked to lie in bed all day. If I wanted something to eat then I bought it and I cooked it daytimes. I read somewhere about a plant that blooms only at night. That was Honey."

I still was unsure. Honey had a little age on her. She'd been through the mill around town. What if this time there'd been no immediate male takers? The need for companionship and financial help might have sent Honey looking elsewhere. Sex is sex. There are many who can't stomach the idea of men with men or women with women. But there are others who can. Maybe Honey, in need, was one of those.

"I've got some other stuff I'm still checking," I said. "You sit tight here and don't give up. Anyone bothering you?"

"No. What kind of deal did the prosecutor offer?"

I told him.

"If I'd done it I'd sure take it. It's a real good offer and I'm grateful to you for getting it for me." He shook his head sadly. "But it wasn't me, Mr. Robak."

"Okay," I said. I'd already begun to believe a little in him. "You sit tight."

He grinned. "I ain't going nowhere. Sheriff came back to see me over the weekend. He said he might let me work outside if I'd give him my solemn promise not to run." He looked down at the floor. "I like Goldie and he knows I wouldn't lie to him. I told him I couldn't promise. Not yet. But maybe I will. He knows if I promise I'll keep the promise."

"Sure," I said. I wasn't going to tell him to promise. It was up to him.

Sheriff Goldie still had his feet up when I came out from the cell area, but the cigar was gone. He motioned me to a chair across from him.

I sat.

"Let me tell you a story that goes back a long time that has to do with things. I was once a kid patrolman for the Bington Police Department and we had us a new judge in town."

"Steinmetz?"

"Sure, Steinmetz. I did all right mostly, but one time I did something I shouldn't have done and I wound up in front of the new judge and he had to hear my case. Some people was out to get me and so I bought me a slick lawyer. You remember old Papannos?"

"I've heard of him, but he was before my time."

"He'd do anything to win a case. But in this one we'd waived a jury and so it went along pretty straight. And they had me dead sure."

I'd been around Bington for years and I'd never heard this story.

"For what?"

"I broke a drunk's jaw. He was a big man in town and I did it cool and without provocation, just because he was a bastard who beat his wife and kids, cheated people, and I bad wanted his jaw broke by me. Four or five witnesses, all *his* people, saw it. And, like I said, they had me except they didn't have me. Not because of the evidence, not because of Papannos, but because of Steinmetz. He saw something in me and he just decided to find me not guilty. The prosecutor raised a lot of hell, the newspapers raised more hell, and the people who was out to get me raised hot blue hell, but there I was, found innocent. And Steinmetz sat upstairs in his big, black chair at the bench and grinned while the hell-raising went on because it was the second year of a six-year term. And it died down and I went back to work as a patrolman, did my twenty plus, and now I'm sheriff. All that happened to me because one man was big enough to believe I'd made a mistake and not committed a crime huge enough to ruin me. I guess I'd do about anything for that man."

"Sure," I said, wondering why I was hearing the story now.

"This can't have nothin' to do with your man Willetts," Goldie continued slowly.

"I'm also looking for Judge Steinmetz's daughter and have been since he was hospitalized. Could it be that it might have something to do with that?"

He gave me a look. "I'd heard you was lookin' for her."

"Tell me what you've got, Goldie. Let me be the judge of it. I feel just now like I'm running out of time on Gail Marie Steinmetz."

"Okay, I'm going to tell you. But you got to promise you won't get into it by representing someone we'd pick up as a result of what you're going to see."

"Other than Stanley and Gail Marie Steinmetz?"

He nodded impatiently. "Sure."

"Agreed."

"You also got to promise me you'll stay shut on this and tell no one else."

"Agreed."

"Do you know John Tom Bertram? He's one of my

deputies. Big as a house, but always grinning and funning."

"I know John Tom." He was the gentlest, nicest deputy sheriff I'd ever known. Maybe six foot five and two hundred and sixty pounds. Sometimes, when I talked and joked with him, I hoped he'd get a little meaner and more careful before he ran onto the wrong person at the wrong time and wound up dead on a dark country road. He was a trusting man and he loved all the world around him. Yet all can't be trusted, all can't be loved.

"Do you know that John Tom's got him a pilot's license and that he likes flying?"

I didn't know that and so I shook my head.

"Well, he do. Sometimes he'll rent him a plane and fly for fun on his off days. Lately he's been doing some flying for me. I pay the freight on the rental, or, actually, the county commissioners do. John Tom watches the river for me and also for the state boys. They got a photo man they send up with him."

I remembered what Detective Lemon had told me in Capitol City. "Drugs," I said.

"Yeah. A lot of drugs on the river these days. Hard to catch. Big boats and barges, lot of them. Got schedules. They come up the river and down the river. Day and night."

"Where's the stuff coming from?"

"Originally from South and Central America. It gets into the states all along the coastline. What we're getting here may be from Memphis or even New Orleans. Just now, according to some D.E.A. gents who've been in and out of her, Bington's the main drop point for Capitol City. The druggers used to road it up, but now there are so many cops, and cars are small and can't carry big loads of Mary Jane. And in cars dogs can sniff it out." He smiled. "Try doing that when you put the package under some coal tonnage. You know where it is and the dogs can't smell it hid deep like that. Get to the drop off point and you go out at night and dig up some coal where you know your package is. John Tom, he and his state buddy, they watch the river. He flies over it lots when the towboat traffic is heavy."

"And you got some photos of what he saw on the river?"

Goldie nodded. "Enough for us to pass on the word to the D.E.A. gents. The next time this particular towboat comes up this way it'll have more eyes on it than a centipede has got legs to fit with pants."

"But why not tell George?"

Goldie shook his head. "Someone up in the feds thinks that there's a man on the B.P.D. who might let the word out. Maybe there is, maybe there ain't. But the D.E.A. wants this one strictly QT until the boat makes another trip upriver." He opened a drawer in his desk and got out a Manila envelope and tossed it across the desk. "Look at these and then give them back."

I opened the package. The first pictures were unremarkable. A big towboat pushed nine loaded coal barges up the river. A second picture was a blowup of the first and, in it, I could make out the name of the pushboat. The *Michael X. Geneva.*

The third picture was of two men in a rowboat not far from the side of the *Michael X. Geneva.* The camera had caught someone aboard the boat signaling to them or throwing something into the river—I couldn't tell for sure which. The men in the boat looked like ordinary river fishermen.

"The drop point was down below Power Plant

Point," Goldie said. "It ain't good fishing there and, on that day, there wasn't another fisherman in sight."

More pictures showed the fishing boat heading into shore.

There were two final pictures. The first showed a vehicle parked off the north side of the river road. It was pulled in under some trees and I couldn't make it out well, but I could see that some kind of odd-appearing vehicle was parked there.

"Now what John Tom does is he'll turn off the motor and come down some and just kind of swoop at what he wants to see. He keeps the shadow of his plane away from them in sun time and his state partner gets a picture or two during the descent," Goldie said. "A couple of times he's got pictures of huge amounts of marijuana, but this packet's so small it's likely cocaine."

The last picture showed the vehicle. The picture was a little sharper than the others. Two men were on shore and they were holding a medium-sized package. Someone in pants and a windbreaker and a hat talked with them in the photo. His/her hand was out to accept delivery. I was fairly sure, without seeing a face, that the deliveree was my friend and onetime client, Sylvia Robinette.

The picture was grainy and indistinct and the photos were all black and whites. I couldn't tell the color of the vehicle. I thought I could make out a face watching from an opened window of the vehicle, a face I'd seen before.

The vehicle, unmistakably, was a Jeep station wagon.

"Do you have a magnifying glass?" I asked Goldie, trying not to be excited.

"Yeah. Someplace." He fumbled in the drawer he'd

gotten the Manila envelope from, cursing amiably but well. He found the glass and handed it to me.

I put the glass on the opened window. The photo was far from conclusive, but I thought the face was that of Gail Marie Steinmetz, *aka* Marie Stone.

"Recognize someone?" Goldie asked cautiously.

"Maybe."

"Good," he said. "I looked careful too. Like I said, I've known the judge for a long time. I knew his wife, God rest her sweet soul, and I knew his daughter that left home young. That's why you're seeing this now, Don, and why I'm taking a chance you'll not embarrass me, you being in the other party and all. That's all I can do for you. And Lord help both of us if the D.E.A.'s find out I've done it."

I looked at the picture once more.

"When was this taken?"

"Last Thursday. Late afternoon. John Tom likes to stay up high and hide in the sun until he glides down."

"Thank you, Goldie," I said humbly. "And you won't hear a word about it. Old silent Robak promises that on his solemn oath."

He smiled and we shook hands.

"Sometime, if it works out, you tell Judge Steinmetz about it. But not for a while. Not till the smoke clears."

"I'll tell him or I'll fix it so you can."

"No, you tell him. In a way I'm still doing something wrong so that something else can come out right. I know I shouldn't do it, but I'm doing it."

I went to the office and called Detective Lemon in Capitol City and caught him at his desk.

"Could I ask you a single question?"

His voice was cool. "Ask."

"Do you have anything up there on a Sylvia Robinette?"

There was silence for a long moment.

"You still there?" I asked.

"I know the name well. I was peripherally involved in a murder case where she was the accused some years ago. She used to half-own and operate a bar up here. She moved down your way a long time back and we lost track of her. I hear around she comes to town now and then, but there's no trouble anymore."

"Was there trouble at one time?"

"She was in the bar business with her husband. Fifteen years or so ago she was indicted for killing him. She got tried and found not guilty by a jury."

"Was she not guilty?"

"Probably guilty, but the case wasn't strong against her and the prosecutor who tried it was brand new and not good at jury trials. The defense lawyer was top-notch. Sylvia and hubby had this bar. One night, when he was drinking heavy, someone put methyl alcohol in his favorite booze bottle when he opened a new one. Here he thought he was drinking out of a brand new bottle of Beefeater Gin and, instead, he was drinking almost straight methyl alcohol. I remember the doc said he was drunk enough already that he couldn't tell or taste or smell the difference. So he poured a lot of it into his glass over ice and drank it straight. Now ethyl alcohol can and will inhibit the poisoning of methyl alcohol, but not in the quantity he drank the methyl alcohol. I was around the crime scene. Methyl alcohol ain't an easy way to go. He was probably semiblind and unable to breathe at the last and the last came quick. I saw him after he was dead and he looked a hundred years old. I think Sylvia delayed calling a doctor or an ambulance until it was too late. She said she just thought he'd passed out. They took her husband to the hospital, but he was DOA, and probably dead while they were loading him. Cool lady. Used to be good-looking, but she'd be sixtyish now. Besides she hated men and liked the ladies. She was into drugs some, but mostly in the sales end through the bar."

"Thank you a lot."

"*De nada*," he said. "I've heard that she comes back around 96th Street now and then, usually with female companions."

I smiled at the telephone receiver. "Did you tell me when I visited that you were Spanish?"

"*Si*. Call me and tell me if you find your judge's daughter. And, by the way, her husband's death was strictly accidental."

"I think I'm getting very close."

I checked with the secretaries. My beautiful nurse had been in and signed her papers in my absence and so I carried them to the courthouse and filed them. The judge was out special judging in another county so I told his court reporter a bit about the case and she typed a note and I signed it so that he'd know about the case and about the expensive car.

I left the courthouse and was walking back when a hunch came to me. Instead of entering the office I got in the Toyota truck and began to tour Bington's automobile row.

I found the orange VW on the third lot I checked. I started out with the local VW-Subaru dealer, and then drove the Toyota to the Ford used car lot. I then found the VW on a used car lot at the back of the Chrysler-Dodge-Plymouth dealer. I parked the truck in a vacant spot and walked to the VW and inspected it. The license had been removed, but a sticker on the trunk of the car indicated that at some time a dealer in Capitol City had owned the car. My inspection also showed me the VW was definitely orange and old and well used.

A mildly curious salesman watched me idly from the sales office window. Eventually he deigned to come out of his air conditioning and approached me.

"Interested?" he asked. "That's a solid old Volks. Lots of good miles left in it if someone wanted it for a second car. Shop in it. Drive it on short trips. It doesn't use much gas." He smiled a professional smile at me. "And cheap. I got better if you'd like to look."

"I see this one used to belong up in Capitol City. How and when did you get it?"

"I took it in trade on a little grey Plymouth a few weeks back."

"Would you give me the name and address of the person who traded the car in to you so that I can contact them about it?"

He looked over at the Toyota truck. "You wanting to trade that truck down?"

I shook my head. "The Toyota's a rental."

He brightened a bit.

"You willing to wait while I see what I can find?"

"Sure. No hurry."

I watched his retreat to air conditioning. The VW door opened to my touch and I got in and looked around. The seats had some holes and the floorboard was worn down to bare metal in a couple of spots. I sat behind the wheel and used my right hand to dig under the front seats.

Nothing.

I slid my hand into the crease between the seat in the

seat back. Nothing again. I decided it might be too much if I started looking in the back seat. I could see the salesman watching me from the window. I was dressed too well to be truly interested in this car and both of us knew it. I gave him my best smile.

He came back out onto the lot eventually. By that time I'd also seen inside the glove compartment. There were a few old maps and some matchbooks. The only place of interest I found on the match folders was that one of them had come from Twiggins Twinkle Club.

"We took that vehicle in trade from a lady named Marie Stone," the salesman said. "Three weeks ago. She traded it in on a 1980 Plymouth. She said her address was 512 W. Main."

512 West Main was Steinmetz's home address.

"Do you remember if anyone was with her when she brought it in to trade?"

The salesman had grown quite edgy. "Why would you want to know that?"

"Do you have a phone I can use?"

"Local call?"

"Yes. To the Bington police." I held up my hand soothingly. "Nothing for you to worry on. Some people are trying to track down the lady who traded in this car."

"She showed the title to it, free and clear."

"It was hers to trade. Again, no problem except we're just trying to find the lady. Can you describe her for me? And also describe anyone who was with her, if you remember anyone."

"She was with a black lady who was a hefty. I remember the trader because I'm a chronic girl watcher. This one wasn't bad-looking, but kind of thin. We got twelve hundred difference and she ironed it off in cash." He looked me over. "You smile extra nice at people who do that."

"Thanks. Now, about that phone?"

He led me inside and let me use his phone. I called George Gentrup.

"I'll come take a look," George said.

"You want me to wait?"

"No. You're to go on now to the hospital. I saw Doc Buckner at breakfast. He said Steinmetz is lots better and that he'd let you stick your nose inside his room for one minute only. I asked if I could go in instead and he said you'd be better than me. I was, of course, highly insulted. But you go."

"I'm on my way right now."

TEN

"Steinmetz's Memoirs" (manuscript) page 178: "I was asked, at that time, to run for judge. I was almost smart enough to refuse, but then one can't always do the right thing."

THE STEINMETZ that I saw on that Monday midmorning was definitely a much-improved Steinmetz. His color was good, his eyes were bright. I could observe that as I entered the intensive care area and looked through the window into Steinmetz's room.

Doc Buckner lurked outside Steinmetz's door. "He said he wanted to see you," he told me bleakly. "He's better, so I reluctantly acceded, but he's not as good as he thinks he is. He also wanted to sit up and so I'm letting him sit up and he wanted to talk and so he's talking." He shook his head wisely. "Now you go in and see him and then you come back out when you see he's getting tired. A couple of minutes inside is all, Robak. I mean it. No more."

"Whatever you say, Doc."

I entered. Steinmetz raised his eyebrows slightly as a greeting.

I took the chair beside his bed and inspected him. He was still wired to monitors and the wires ran from him up to the ceiling.

"Don't bother to ask how I'm doing," he said in a low voice.

I could detect no slurring of speech and he rubbed one hand over the other and then switched hands to complete the job. "They're going to start some light therapy with me day after tomorrow for my legs." His brow clouded. "And, Don boy, they say no drinking at all!"

"For how long?"

"For them, forever. For me, only until I'm out of this place," Steinmetz said craftily, lowering his voice so that Doc Buckner couldn't hear him.

"Have you got a will?" I asked. "I mean one you've executed?"

"Sure I have. Typed it up myself at home. An original and a copy."

"Where is it?"

"The copy's in my grey storage box in the drawer in the study. The original is hid in a plastic wrapper and taped to the lower side of the bathtub, on the side clos-est to the window and the wall in the bathroom. I hid it there one night after reading a private eye novel, like I told you a couple of times before."

"You told me you'd hidden it there?"

"Sure I did." He watched my face. "At least I think I did. Maybe I forgot. When you asked me where it was a minute ago I thought you were just checking my mem-ory. I didn't tell you?"

"No."

"How about my daughter?"

"I'm close. I'll find her soon. The question is what do you want me to do when I have found her?"

"See what she needs. See if she'll take my help. I ran her off and so maybe she no longer wants anything to do with me." He frowned, thinking. "Fifteen years is a long time gone. But no one gets any of my money by putting a note in my mailbox."

"Where are your stock certificates?"

"In the packet with the bathtub will. Are you sure I didn't tell you about the will?"

"You didn't." I thought for a moment. "One more thing: Do you owe any money to that Mrs. Milton who worked for you?"

"Not a dime. I paid her by check every week. The bank will have a record. Every check is marked 'payment in full to date.' I've defended too damned many unfounded claims in estates not to take due care. I did leave her a chunk in my estate and intend her to get that. Is she claiming I owe her money?"

"I don't know. I've not yet seen her. Her son said she was off visiting people. But something he said after that made me wonder."

"That fat lout. He's been in prison across the river and my bet is he'll make it again. I fired his mother because she got to the point where she was trying to run my life. I further got rid of her because she insisted he bring her over to work and then pick her up when she was done. I didn't like seeing him parked in front of my house or at my door to pick her up. Ruined the appearance of the neighborhood. I didn't like the guns in his back window and I didn't like all his gut muscle." He smiled at me and showed me he had his false teeth in place. "I further fired her because I think she wanted me to marry her. She kept bringing marriage up. At my age my interest in women is a watcher's interest only. So I fired her and hired someone else."

"Who did you hire?" I asked, thinking I knew.

"A younger lady named Ruby Willetts. She came to

me about a divorce and wanted to work out the fee. So I hired her and then that crazy, jailbird husband of hers supposedly killed her. She was only at the house to clean once. Did a good job and besides she was much prettier than Mrs. Milton."

"Maybe her husband killed her, maybe not," I said.

"Ah hah, you're representing him?"

I nodded.

Steinmetz looked around his small domain. "I want out of here quick. Doc says best wait. He also says that when I go I'll need round-the-clock nurses. I suppose that's okay as long as they're pretty ones."

"You want pretty ones?" I said, thinking of one.

"Sure."

Buckner motioned to me from the door.

"I'd better leave now."

"Find her, Don."

"I can almost promise for sure I will. Someone may have taken the will copy. Is it okay with you if I pick up the stuff behind your bathtub and put it in a bank lock-box in your name?"

"That's okay."

I got up and walked to the door.

"You've tired him a little," Buckner said severely. "But now maybe he'll sleep some more. He needs lots of rest. Did he ask you to sneak him in any booze?"

"No. Not yet anyway."

Buckner frowned. "He's not as well as I'd thought."

"That's not it. He's waiting for discharge. How soon will that be?"

"Who knows for certain. Even when he gets out of here he'll need total care until he goes through a lot of therapy. I don't think the one leg will ever come all the way back. He can't walk, Robak."

"Doc, old pal, did you ever see a wheelchair in a bar?"
Buckner nodded gloomily. "I understand what you
mean."

I went to Steinmetz's house. I went inside and
checked for the grey box in the study again. I thought,
momentarily, that maybe a mistake had been made, and
that on this day I'd find the box and the will copy that
Steinmetz said he'd placed there. In the drawer I found
miscellaneous papers, old newspaper clippings mostly,
things I'd seen when I checked before. There was still
no grey box and no will copy. Someone had come into
the house and taken them and left only the junk in the
drawer.

I went to the front of the house and looked out one of
the tiny windows that opened to the street. I wondered
if I was being watched. I saw nothing. Yet I was uneasy.
And I had learned to trust in my instincts.

I checked the inside of the house carefully. It was
empty.

The old, porcelain tub stood on four clawed legs in
the bathroom. By getting all the way down on the floor
and against the wall I could see a package hanging
down on the lower side of the tub.

I had a feeling that kept running up and down my
backbone like someone was walking on my grave. I
started to reach a hand back in along the tub and pull
the package off. Then I decided not to do it.

I went to the phone instead.

I took off the speaker and looked inside the phone. If
it was being tapped it wasn't being done simply, but I
wasn't sure it wasn't being tapped.

If the person or persons who'd gotten the will copy
(and surely seen it was a copy and not the original) was

watching, he'd not yet found the will original and stock
certificates.

I called my office and checked out for the day. I told
them I'd be in tomorrow morning.

I then went into the kitchen. I found scissors and a
plastic bag. I cut old newspapers into strips, used rub-
ber bands I found in a drawer to hold them, and put the
resultant packet into the plastic bag.

I opened and then closed Steinmetz's front door. I
stood in the front yard and looked around me.

It was opening time at some nearby swimming pool,
probably the public one above the river. Kids in swim-
suits, carrying towels, kept walking past me and turning south at the next corner. Even in the shade of the
trees the heat was oppressive and so I stood and
watched around me and smelled the river a few blocks
away.

Across the street, a block down, I saw a grey Plymouth. It was parked along the street and I couldn't see
anyone inside. There were big trees along the street on
both sides and someone could be watching me from behind one of them.

I hefted the plastic bag carefully, trying to keep it out
of sight, and yet hold it so it could be noticed.

The Toyota truck was hot inside. I rolled up the windows after I turned on the air conditioning to its highest setting. I put the package on the seat beside me.

As I drove away two vehicles pulled away from the
curbs behind me. One was the grey Plymouth. It made
a U-turn in wide Main Street. The other car was a Jeep
station wagon.

Maybe the thing to do was to drive to George Gentrup's police station, but my followers were doing no
wrong and I had nothing so far except a lot of hunches.

Driving there might scare them off and I wasn't sure that was what I wanted.

I drove on out of town and found the river road, the one that eventually would take me to Sylvia Robinette's farm.

Somewhere, on the drive, I lost them. At least I was alone when I parked off the road a mile away from Sylvia's farm retreat. I hid the truck key and my bogus papers under the floor mat.

I walked. When I heard someone coming I darted off the road and hid where I could. I'd not been walking long until both the Plymouth and the Jeep station wagon passed me, moving fast, drivers not looking right or left. I could see women inside the vehicles from my hiding point, but could make out no faces.

When those two vehicles had passed me I stayed above the road. It wasn't bad walking now. Dry weather had firmed up the earth and I could trudge along without leaving heavy tracks. The earth was still moist, but it was drying fast. Birds flew and insects buzzed around me. In a few days the courthouse farming brigade would again be watching the skies for rain. For a farmer life is always too much rain or too little rain. One farmer once told me he was like an alcoholic, too wet or too dry.

I found the entrance to Sylvia's farm and bypassed it carefully, not wanting to enter there. A few hundred yards past I jumped the drainage ditch by the road and made my way through the underbrush to the grove of trees and bushes where I'd watched before.

Both vehicles were parked in front of the house and I wondered at the why on that. The door to the barn was partially closed. Why were the cars out instead of in the barn?

I settled in and watched patiently. The day wore on. I missed lunch and then dinner. The sun fell low without there being any activity other than the activity of the insects, birds, and animals close to me.

No one came out of the house. No one did anything. Lights in the house, on all three floors, came on. I waited for the blinds to be drawn, but on this night they stayed open.

I wanted to get in closer.

I moved out of my grove of trees and bushes. I paused for a moment at the edge of my place of concealment and thought things over. Maybe I had a tribe of ladies up there awaiting me. That could be the reasons the blinds had been left open, an open invitation for a long-nosed, aging lawyer. *Come into my parlor, stupid fly.*

My curiosity won out. I could always run from them, find my way to the railroad cut, and make the top of the hill on the other side of Sylvia's house. I remembered that Sylvia was also a runner. I'd seen her run and perhaps she was better than me, but Sylvia alone? I thought I was at least a physical match for her unless she managed to wing me with her shotgun or a bottle of bogus Beefeater.

I just had to look inside the lighted windows. Somewhere close was Steinmetz's daughter.

I moved along carefully and silently.

Why were the cars parked outside instead of in the barn, I asked myself again? Maybe something else was now in the barn. Was that it?

I drew close enough to look into the first-floor windows of the house and see small portions of the inside. I saw furniture and mirrors. I saw nothing else. I decided

they were on one of the upper floors. Someone had to
have turned the lights on.

I decided to peek inside the barn while I was this
close.

I walked softly toward the partially open door and
stepped inside its deeper darkness. In a corner there
were small bags of something I'd not seen there before.
I walked that way.

"Just hold it right where you are, Robak," Sylvia said
from somewhere near in the darkness.

I bolted for the door. A dark shadow struck at me
with something round and hard. A club of some kind. It
ricocheted heavily off my shoulder and caught me in the
head and I was down.

I could make out four women above me.

Sylvia seemed to smile down at me. "There's an auto-
matic switch that turns on the lights in the house when
it's set. We set it early this morning. We've been waiting
for you most of the day. I told you not to come back
before, but then we found your tracks. They were your
tracks, weren't they Robak?"

"Not mine." I sat up.

"I believe they were and so do my girls. I know you
know one of them, although you've not seen her for a
number of years." She nodded at the thinnest of the
three girls. "This is Gail Marie Steinmetz, now known
as Marie Stone. She's with us, Robak."

I looked Gail Marie over. She was thinner than I remembered her, but she didn't look bad. Her hands
shook a little and her eyes seemed tired. She looked
down at the ground in front of her, not meeting my
eyes.

"She's been sick, but of course you know about that.
She's better now. She'll be better than ever once we

locate any other copies of her father's will. We have a copy. Somewhere there's an original. Is that what you carried out of the judge's house earlier, Robak?"

I said nothing.

A large black girl stood near Gail Marie. She watched me without a change of expression. I saw the weapon she'd hit me with. It was a baseball bat.

"This is Wanda Carson. She and Gail Marie are best friends. The other young lady in jeans is Judy Torpin. Judy's a friend to everyone female."

Judy smiled.

"Which one of them was a friend to Honey Willetts?" I asked. "Or was that you, Sylvia?"

If my question disturbed anyone I couldn't discern it.

"In case you've all forgotten, she's the lady who went to work for the judge when he fired another lady just before you people put the note in his mailbox."

"We've decided a lot of money is worth more than a little money," Sylvia said. "Isn't that right, girls? The judge dies without a will and daughter here gets his dollars. With his money we can build the kingdom here some more, put some high, electrified fences around this place. Gail Marie, of course, wants to share her good fortune with her friends."

I wasn't going to say anything about drugs. Let them find out that the D.E.A. and Sheriff Goldie were onto them. I tried to look confused.

"You've already got money, Sylvia. What do you want with a little more of Judge Steinmetz's?"

"It isn't a little. And my trust fund was an insurance deal set up by my late husband and runs out next January. I spent it all. Back to the cold. Back to being a peon. I won't do it, Robak." She smiled at me and I decided she was probably insane, but that it wasn't the kind of insanity that would ever benefit me.

"You're going to get us in the hospital, Robak. You're going to help the four of us in to see Judge Steinmetz. You saw him. Surely his daughter and her friends can see him also. There we're going to tell him what his daughter is. We'll let Wanda Carson and Marie show him. You think he'll survive that, Robak?"

He probably would. In his years on the bench Steinmetz claimed he'd seen almost all. But this woman thought that seeing his daughter as a lesbian would kill him. And she thought that I could take her into his room. The whole thing sounded like a drug dream.

"You take me back into town to the hospital and you can bet I'll manage to get done what I want done and not what you want done."

She smiled. "We're not going to take you. You're going to write a note to him about his daughter. The note might get Wanda and Marie past the guard. If not, then we'll improvise. We'll take you in the house now. I want you to write a note to the judge's doctor. We'll hold you for a time until you become more willing to do that. I've some things which will aid us in your compliance. Gail Marie will also make a tearful call to her father or whoever answers for him. Once we get in I guarantee we'll not go out until Judge Steinmetz gets the full story on his daughter."

"I think his will cuts her out."

"Not fully. He leaves her some money. A pittance. And we think you have the original. Without a will she inherits all. So I'm going to send Judy and Marie down to find your truck. When they find it they'll rescue the documents and we shall make a bonfire of those we don't need. And we'll put your truck where we put your car after we went completely over it. In the river."

"I had insurance, Sylvia. Were you in a fit of pique when you took my car?"

"It seemed the thing to do. It might have stopped your looking, but you stayed nosy. Go find his truck vehicle, Marie. Take Judy with you."

She stepped away from me and Judy Torpin and Gail Marie followed. In a few moments I heard a motor start out in the drive and I was left with only Wanda Carson and Sylvia as my guards.

And so we waited for a time.

My strength had come back. The buzzing in my head had abated and, although I was sore, I thought I'd have no trouble running.

I waited for a chance.

It came when the car came back. I heard the motor. Sylvia watched me intently, her old eyes glistening. Wanda Carson was completely impassive, but she held tight to her bat.

They heard the car a second after I did. They turned away from me. They went to the only opening in the barn. I gathered my feet underneath me and came up at a run. I tried to go between them. They made no room, but I almost made it. I was out the door when the bat or the gun butt caught me. I saw it coming a little and I tried to make it miss, but it didn't miss completely.

I lay on the ground. Sylvia and the others talked, but I couldn't make out a word. I did understand that they'd found the Toyota truck and left it behind when they'd found nothing other than the newspaper clippings in the plastic bag.

I hurt.

I started to come back just a little, but I lay there on the ground and listened. And now I could hear.

"This guy's a smart ass," Sylvia said. "Win or lose, when this thing is done he dies for sure. We played a game with him and he played a game on us. So now he dies. And I'll be the one to do it."

ELEVEN

"Steinmetz's Memoirs" (manuscript) page 209: "The best advice I can give when trouble begins is keep low and make sure your powder is dry."

THE ROOM where the four of them dropped me was on the third floor. I came a tiny bit further back to consciousness, but I stayed limp and let them haul me as dead weight up the steps. I was large enough for it to be a chore.

Wanda cursed me all the way up. Judy only grunted when she had to lift much. Sylvia was strong and had fallen silent for now after her death threats. Gail Marie was more in the way than a help. She carried ropes from the barn to tie me and they brushed against me once or twice. Twine of some kind. Maybe it was old. I remembered that Sylvia hadn't worked the farm for a long time.

They dropped me on a floor that smelled both of dust and strong cleaning compounds.

Sylvia said, "Tie him and tie him good. He gets conscious, then there's some questions we need to have him answer. We need the will. Once we get it we need inside the hospital and then we need Robak dead."

I'd hoped that Gail Marie would bind me, but Wanda did the honors. She got my hands first and I kept my wrist muscles as rigid as I could. She failed to notice and worked her knots behind me until the cords were tight enough, even with muscles rigid, to begin to cut off circulation.

When she'd finished with my wrists then she went at my ankles. I was afraid she'd notice if I tried making muscles there and so I stayed limp. Once, for Wanda's benefit, I moaned heavily without moving.

Sylvia's voice sounded satisfied once I was well trussed. "He's still out and I think he'll remain that way for a time. I want him awake and alert before I go to work on him with my little treasure trove of drugs. After I get done and we get what we want, there's a place we can take him, weight him, and get rid of him. Deep and dark and wet." She paused and then said it again, evidently liking the phrase. "Deep and dark and wet."

Gail Marie made a little sigh.

"What's the matter with you?" Sylvia asked.

"I knew him when I was real young is all."

"You going to put him in the river?" Wanda asked Sylvia, interested.

"Sure. The river. But a special place where they don't fish and he can lay deep and silent."

Gail Marie sighed again.

"You girls watch him close, Gail Marie. We need him, but only for a while. He may realize that when he wakes up. He's had some trouble before. Some folks around here tell tales about him. I think he's trickier than he looks to be. I sure don't want him getting loose."

"He doesn't know anything about us and what we're doing," Judy said.

"He knows you're here. He could pick you out of a lineup book. With that the cops might get onto what we're doing here, both things, Steinmetz and the other."

They went to the room door and I heard it open. They stopped there and whispered for a moment and I couldn't make out what they whispered about.

Then Sylvia said: "I don't think you can hear me, Robak, but I'm sorry we got to do to you what we will do. But none of you men things are worth a solitary damn, not from the husband who mistreated me until I killed him to the cops who put me in a dark cell for doing it. I beat those cops and got found innocent. And now I've beaten you. None of you are worth a solitary damn."

I heard the door close.

I own a phobia about being tied up. It's medium strong. Phobias are common enough so that many people have one or more. I once knew a man well who lived in the same place for all his life, leaving it only when compelled, living in the hell such leaving created for those brief times he positively had to be outside his home. I've known people who fear elevators, heights, blood, death, and the like.

I cannot abide ropes that tie me. Once, when I was very young, someone did tie and leave me in a dark place. I think it was a game, but it was quickly not a good game for me. The memory of being tied remains with me as does the name of the boy who tied me. He died in a war and I remember I wasn't immediately sorry when I heard it.

All I can remember now about being tied that time are the ropes, the black place of the confinement, and fighting and tearing until I was bloodily free.

As soon as I'd heard them away, even though I was

still groggy and my coordination was poor, I began to try to get the hated ropes off me.

She'd tied my arms a little high and, when I relaxed my arm muscles, the ropes around my arms were still tight, but blood made it through and my hands remained workable. I managed to work the ropes down lower to the place on my wrists where skin and muscle and bones were thinnest.

I looked around the room. There was an old, single bed with a mattress, not made up, no sheets or covering. There was a rickety bureau. There was a battered night table.

I rolled over to the edge of the bed and looked underneath. It was a spring bed and the springs were tired and rusty. The mattress above was thin and smelled of mold.

Several springs had buckled and broken. That had left sharp ends. I found the best one and explored it with my wrists, having to turn over on my stomach to accomplish it. I was unable then to see the springs, but I could feel them. I tried running the sharp spring end into the knots on my wrists with only minor success.

I kept working at it. The twine was tough and stiff and, I thought, old. It had been wound around my wrists and then looped and tied finally into a complicated knot. The loops around my ankles were tight enough to cause me to begin to lose all feeling in my feet as I worked at my wrists.

The sharp spring was pointed only on the free end. It wasn't of use for cutting because it was round. But I could use the end to pierce and tear at the knots. I kept getting my wrists up to it awkwardly and then trying to push the sharp end through the biggest knot. Most times the point failed to pierce the knot and instead jabbed me. In a while my wrists grew slippery with my own blood, but I felt I was making progress.

I turned over on my back and looked again at the puzzle that faced me. I moved closer to the bed. It was too low at the side to let me slide under, but it wasn't heavy. I turned back over, put my head under the outer rail, and lifted the bed off the floor. I tried hard to make no noise.

I now was facedown on the floor and partly under the bed. I found the sharp point with my wrists and shoved and withdrew. I did it clumsily a hundred times and then five hundred and then a thousand. I felt the ropes around my wrist beginning to give a little.

I heard someone coming down the hall. It was too late to try to get out from under the bed so I lay there motionless hoping that my efforts would not be noticed, but knowing for certain that they would.

Gail Marie opened the door and looked in. She saw me and her mouth opened. I thought she was going to call for help. I watched her. She shook her head at me and put her finger to her lips.

She stepped back into the hall and called loudly: "He's okay. Looks like he's still unconscious." She pulled the door shut behind her.

I had no time to try to understand. I jabbed more and felt the twine fray and I kept at the jabbing and jerking and picking, now in a frenzy of motion, push, pull, push. The pain was nothing. The desire to escape the ropes was everything.

Then it was done. The twine parted and there was enough room made for me to use my hands to tear away the rest.

Unloosing my ankles was easy, but my feet were now

a bad problem. I was dead below the ankles. After I removed the twine I couldn't stand.

Soon someone other than Gail Marie would come to check on me.

I crawled to the door. It wasn't tightly fastened and I eased it open an inch or two. Down the hall there was a lighted room. Judy Torpin sat in a chair by the door. She was doing her toenails, painting them a bright red.

No exit out that way.

I eased the door closed again and silently crawled to the single window. I pulled myself up and stood on still useless feet. Then a thousand needles inside them began to happen, not yet hurting, but there. The window curtain had been closed by someone and so I parted it. I could see outside. The night was brightened by half a moon and there seemed to be few clouds. For now nothing obscured that moon.

The window opened to my pushes without any loud sounds. I stood framed in the breeze that blew in. I looked down. The ground was thirty feet away, too far to jump. Above me and out I could see the edge of the roof. The guttering that hung from that edge seemed solid-looking and well attached. Up here on the third floor the ceiling was lower. I wondered, if I lowered the upper window down and managed to climb out, if I could then reach the gutters. Twenty feet away, to my right, there was a down drain, huge and old and appearing rock solid.

I sat down for a moment and furiously rubbed my feet, trying to work circulation into them. In a while I could feel them very well as they ached and stung. I tried standing again. I was tottery, but I stood. I lowered both windows so that the top half of the window stood open. I stepped first up onto the window sill and then on up to the ledge the open upper window made above the sill. Above me the moon was now blotted out by the overhanging roof. The bricks in the wall were slippery where I touched them, with old moss and ivy. I held on inside the window top and leaned back touching the underside of the eave. I leaned back as far as I could and felt the underside of the guttering. I raised on tiptoe and stretched high. I caught the rim of the gutter. I let go with my feet and swung out.

The old gutter, which had looked substantial, wasn't. It creaked ominously. I went along it hand over hand to the down pipe.

In seconds I was on the ground. My feet were still partly dead and felt as if they were undirectable. The right foot kept buckling beneath me so that I made slow progress.

By the light of the moon I could see the railroad cut far away. I walked slowly that way.

Above me, when I was a hundred feet in back of the house, I saw a light come on in the room I'd escaped. A loud voice yelled in rage. *Wanda.*

I couldn't run yet, but I lengthened my stride and walked away from the house as quickly as I could manage.

I tried to keep trees between me and the house. When I was two hundred feet away I heard them come bursting onto the back porch. I stepped behind a tree and took both cover and a backward look. They stood looking out. I saw that Sylvia had a shotgun and Wanda carried a pistol.

Sylvia cursed. She turned to Judy and said, "Get a flashlight from the closet in the living room. He can't be far. We've got to find him. Don't give him a chance. Kill him if you see him. We'll burn that old house of

Steinmetz's. Maybe the will's in there somewhere. Then we'll wait and see what happens."

I stayed behind the sheltering tree and then found others. I let them block me from sight as best they could. I kept moving. In another few hundred feet I was in deep underbrush. I found I could run a little now and so I did, getting better at it all the time in spite of the gimpy right ankle.

I heard Sylvia once more from far away. "He'll probably head for the railroad cut. It's a way up. I can run him down if he does that. The only other thing he might do is try the river road. Judy, you go with Wanda along the road. Take the car. If you see him shoot him. I'm going for the cut. If I get there before he does or catch up with him on it, I'll take him." Her voice sounded confident.

One of the others muttered a protest, but Sylvia ignored it. "Do what I tell you," she said. "How'd you not see he was getting away, Gail Marie?"

"He was all tied up," Gail Marie said. "Don't blame me. I didn't tie him."

"He gets to the sheriff and we're all in deep trouble. You go with the others, Marie. I'll go by myself."

I ran on, but the right ankle wasn't right. It was stiff and sore, as if I'd unknowingly, when it was dead, turned it badly. I had no idea when I'd done it, but it was done and it impeded me. Still, I ran.

The railroad cut was half a mile away. With luck I could reach it first and be far enough ahead of Sylvia to have a chance to make it to the top without getting shotgunned. And, at the top, I knew the land and the quarries. The river road might have been better, but the land in front of the house was mostly open fields. I was glad I'd not gone that way.

I found myself a tree and I stopped on the shadow side and listened. At first all I heard was the wind that had begun to come up. Then I heard something else. I knelt and put an ear to the ground and listened. Over the sound of the wind I heard footsteps. Someone approached, running.

I got up, but stayed where I was, listening and watching. The half-moon ducked in and out of clouds and my ankle throbbed.

I saw Sylvia come out into a patch of moonlight. She was running quickly, moving well. I thought I was maybe even with her, but it was hard to judge because she was following a different, and perhaps easier, path than I ran. And I saw she was moving far faster than I could now run.

I controlled my panic and did some thinking. Maybe it was better to let her get to the cut first. She was going to do it anyway. If she got there she might presume that I was still ahead of her. Maybe she'd speed on up the cut. *Or maybe she'd lie in wait.*

I saw her again moments later. She'd slowed her pace and then I saw her stop in the open and listen. I stayed in my shadows. In a while she ran on again. She was carrying her shotgun. She looked impatient to use it.

If I stayed where I was, chances were they'd catch me come daybreak. If I continued for the cut, then Sylvia would now run on up it and lay in wait for me. If I tried going back the other way, then there were two or three others. If Gail Marie was my ally, I couldn't count on her being a helpful one.

A night bird sang and the warm wind rustled the leaves of the tree beside me.

I changed tactics. Instead of running I walked. That cut down noise. I no longer huffed and puffed. And I

had time to think and remember about the land on top
of the hill.

The cut had been constructed prior to the Civil War
in the days of rail expansion. It was steep, but noncog
steep. Because it was steep and narrow, rain had always
been a problem. A heavy rain could wash away roadbed
gravel and loosen ties. So, I remembered from hearing a
local historian, for maintenance purposes the railroad
had opened small sidecuts at right angles to the rails.
There, in the halcyon days of rail travel, gravel and railroad ties had been stored. And when trains rumbled up
and down the cut, north and south, the railroad workers
could use these alcoves to escape the dangers of the used
right-of-way.

There were four such places. If I could get to the
third on up the hill without Sylvia shotgunning me,
then I thought I might know something about it that
she didn't.

I walked. In walking I searched for and used darker
places. I prayed for clouds to cover the moon, but the
sky remained mostly clear.

I reached the bottom of the cut and looked up. The
grade was steep. A mile plus away, lost in darkness, was
the top of the cut.

I listened. Sylvia wouldn't know about my ankle. She
might now be anyplace along the rail cut or at the top. I
heard nothing in the listening. From my experience
with her as client and captor I thought she was a great
believer in her own abilities. I thought she'd be certain
she'd outrun me, having not heard me ahead. And so, in
one of the sidecuts or at the top, she'd wait silently for
me, shotgun at ready. I thought she'd killed before and
doing me in wasn't something that she'd worry on. She
needed me, but now she needed me dead because I had

escaped. She'd not take a chance on that happening again.

I stayed off the gravel where I could. The railroad no longer maintained the track because it was now not in use, but gravel remained, washed down from higher up. I walked up disintegrating ties and smelled the smells of rotting wood and rusting steel.

The first cut was bone empty. All the gravel was gone. I looked around the corner into the opening, ready to take quick flight if Sylvia was there, but the cut was as empty as a Sunday morning wine bottle.

I continued on. Perspiration ran down my back. Now and then I stopped and listened. I heard night sounds. An owl hooted above me. Night bugs buzzed around my head, feeding on me while I was still warm.

I was very careful at the second cut. I edged into the opening. The moon picked that moment to go behind a cloud. My heart leaped inside me, but my eyes could see even in the deep darkness by now. I listened and watched.

The cut was empty. I let out my breath.

I moved on. The next sidecut was the crucial one. It lay a quarter mile below the final sidecut, but only a hundred feet below it in altitude. Above the third sidecut the tracks leveled out.

I thought that if I waited for someone I'd have chosen sidecut three. But Sylvia was Sylvia.

The cloud left the moon.

I moved on.

Near the third cut entrance I put my ear to the stones and listened for a time. I heard nothing.

I looked inside the cut, first from one side, and then, by darting across, from the other. A small pile of gravel and a few railroad ties were all that I saw. Behind them was the hill.

Someone had built little steps up from the back of the sidecut to the top of the hill. I'd discovered them by chance in a winter run when the underbrush had withered and no longer hidden the steps.

The third cut was vacant. I walked to the back of it and took the steps upward. They lay at an almost ninety degree angle away from the railroad cut itself. But there came a time, as I climbed, that I was outlined against the sky. Someone, looking from atop the cut could see me.

That someone did.

I saw the flash of light and heard the explosion as I began to run. I forgot my bad ankle and sprang up and away, doing the steps three at a time, knowing that I might fall. If I did then all chance died. I heard another shot and buckshot buzzed past my ears.

I made the top of the hill.

Sylvia followed.

On top I knew the land. I knew the quarries. The area, for miles now, was limestone country. There were a few small caves, but mostly unused quarries full of water from underground springs plus some wasteland and some woodland. Anything that grew up on top grew oddly and poorly because the ground was rocky.

I ran flat out.

Sylvia pursued. I could hear her behind me. I ran, beginning to hurt a little, but still all right.

Ahead lay the Big N Quarry. I knew it well from swimming there. I hoped Sylvia did not know it. Maybe she did and I was dead.

The Big N was called that because it resembled that letter in configuration. Busy limestone workers had emptied it of most of its commercial grade limestone in the fifties and sixties and let it fill with water. It was a good place to spend a summer day. The water was clear and cool. In some places it was a hundred feet deep, but in others piles of noncommercial stones lay only a few feet under the surface. Daytime swimming was fairly safe except for the rash and foolish. At night swimming and diving into any quarry was as dangerous as a nest of copperhead snakes.

I was going to take a little swim. I remembered a place where I could dive into deep water and then swim to a shelter in the huge stones. If my memory was correct, for Sylvia to get at me she'd have to follow behind. If she chose the safe way around the quarry, then I could swim into hiding while she did so and exit at any of a dozen places and lose her.

Because I knew where things were, I wanted her to see me make my leap and then have her jump from what she thought was the same place.

I heard her behind me. I was at a set of jumbled, huge stones. I thought and hoped they were the ones I knew. It was difficult to tell in the light.

I rose against the rocks and heard her yell.

"You stop, Robak. I don't want to kill you. Stop." And then the gun went off again. I heard buzzing in the night.

I jumped off the highest stone. I didn't jump straight out, but instead I jumped sideways to another stone six feet below and then, sideways from that. I hit the cool water. It stung the open places on my wrists. I stroked quickly over and rose into water-level stone and entered the alcove those huge, low stones created.

By that time she was at my first rock and looking for me. She shot down towards me, but I was inside the stones and I heard the buckshot ricochet off the face of the limestone blocks.

She stood atop the upper limestone blocks and cursed me.

"Come out of there, you nosy bastard. Come out and I'll let you live."

I laughed at her from inside my shelter and she heard the laughter.

"I'm coming after you. When I get you I'll shoot off your legs, one at a time. Then I'll finish you, but only after you've hurt for a long time."

I couldn't see her. But I knew there was no way down to where I was except through water or by going around the quarry.

I called out, "I've got some big rocks for you. Get close and maybe I'll chunk you with one."

I heard her jump. Straight out. In the dark water out there was a huge, pointed stone, setting two feet below the water line. It was a place where a young girl had once died. I knew that.

I heard her hit. Then no sound. No sound at all.

I went to the opening of my stones and looked out carefully.

Her head was up out of the water. The shotgun had gone deep. Her old eyes sought me.

"Stay away," she whispered.

The blunt point of the rock had taken her low in the belly and she was impaled on it.

I went into the water and swam to her.

She watched me all the way.

"I'll help you."

"No. No you won't. None of you ever did."

"Why did you kill Honey Willetts?" I asked.

She shook her head angrily, closed her eyes, and died.

I got her off the point and onto the rocks so that she'd not sink. I then swam on around and found a spot where I could climb out on the other side. I squeezed out the excess water from my clothes as well as I could, put them back on, and then ran. An hour later I found a farmhouse and called Sheriff Goldie and George Gentrup from there.

TWELVE

*"Steinmetz's Memoirs" (manuscript) page 342 (final page):
"No matter what the question, the answer at my age is always
'I ain't dead yet.'"*

THEY PLACED ALL of Sylvia's trio of assistants in jail because Sheriff Goldie, after I related the events of
Sylvia's last night, thought his plans might be best
served that way. I swore to him that I'd not talked about
drugs, asked no questions about drugs, and that drugs
had played no part in what had happened to me. The
ladies had taken me because I was the key to Steinmetz
and not for any other reason. I told Goldie about the
bags I'd seen in the barn, but that I'd never discussed
them or asked any questions about them.

On the second day after my big run I visited the
women's section of the jail after getting an okay from
Goldie. Wanda Carson was the one I wanted to see first.

She sat in her cell and watched me and I tried to read
her dark eyes, but that wasn't possible. She merely sat
on her cot in the women's part of the jail watching out
the bars, composed, waiting.

"The sheriff wants me to sign an information against
you for battery with a deadly weapon. I'm thinking
some on it. You whopped me around pretty good,

Wanda. I still get the dizzies now and then when I get up too quick."

She waited silently. She smiled a meaningless smile.

"If I decided I didn't want to sign an information like that what would you do when you got out of this jail?"

That brought a single word from her: "Why?"

"I was thinking that if you went back to Capitol City alone or with Judy I just might not sign a felony information. If you were figuring on talking Gail Marie into going along with you I just might sign the papers."

"What happens if she wants to come?"

"Then she can follow along later. Right now I want her checked out by a doctor. I want her to see her father."

"Ain't nothin' bad wrong with Marie."

"If that checks out then I want her to see her father very soon."

"This set-up and plan wasn't her idea. Someone come to Capitol City and talked to her. Someone I didn't know. No one ever told me who it was. Marie, she got told that she ought to get back down here because her father was sick and was about to get took for some money." She looked up at the ceiling of the cell. "We got down here around Bington and I knew Sylvia from a long time back so we went to call on her. One thing led to another and Sylvia took the thing over, did the thinking and planning, wrote out the notes and all. And we was living on Sylvia at her place, her food, her booze and stuff. I liked that okay so her taking charge was okay also."

"Gail Marie doesn't look good."

"Too much drugs, but she don't hardly needle none now. She still drinks too much booze. She's a lot better than she was when we was up in Capitol City 'cause

Sylvia took her in hand. Sylvia made her run mornings. Had her up to two miles. Had her eatin' good and makin' sense when she talked most times."

"Would you want out of here on like a fine and a short suspended sentence?"

"Sure." She watched me carefully, now trying to read me. "Can I come back?"

"Okay with me. I wouldn't and couldn't stop you from coming back. I'm a lawyer and not a cop. And I can't stop Gail Marie from finding you once this is over."

"No. I think maybe it's done. It never was much between us. She wasn't happy being a woman's woman. She lost her man in an accident and I happened onto her. I bought her drugs and I got her booze. She was a hog for them things and so she stayed with me." She smiled at me without real malice. "Way it was, Sylvia run things at that farm. I took whatever orders she gave. She said crack you and so I cracked you. And if I'd caught you out on the road that night I would have shot you. But I ain't Sylvia. I don't hate men. I just don't use them." She smiled again, another smile without meaning.

"Sylvia's getting buried tomorrow. I heard today from the sheriff that they were putting her in the ground next to where she buried her husband," I said.

"She'll roll forever in that grave. How'd you do what you did to her? She had the big power. She was strong and smart and she hated real good. How'd you get out of them ropes I tight tied and then do the job you did on Sylvia?"

"I'm not telling. You might catch me again. Or you might decide to come back here after me and I'd need to get away or come after you."

She shivered just a little. "No, man. I ain't foolin' with you no more. I tied you hog-tight and you got out and got Sylvia. I hear your name in something I'm into, and I'm through the alley, headin' out. It ain't smart to fool with someone who's got more power than Sylvia. She like to kill people. She killed a couple of men before she done for that old, mean husband of hers and no one ever caught up with her. I heard her brag on it." She grinned, savoring the idea. "And now she be buried next to her old man?"

"Yes."

"She might come back after you for that."

I thought of something I wanted to check out. I no longer believed that Honey Willetts had ever been around Sylvia and the rest. I got out my picture of her and I handed it to Wanda in her cell. She took it in her dry, warm, and massive hand.

"You know this one?" I asked.

"No. I ain't never seen her before."

I believed her. *I was pretty sure I knew who did know her.*

And so Wanda and I made a deal. On the following day she and Judy paid small fines and costs in county court, took thirty days each suspended on a charge of simple battery, and then drove away. They took the grey Plymouth with a note from Gail Marie allowing it. And I delivered Gail Marie first to Doc Buckner and then we all drove to the hospital. Buckner looked her over there, thought it was okay, and so I left father and daughter alone together in Steinmetz's room.

She was inside with him for a few minutes. Doc Buckner watched from the door and I watched through the window. Things seemed to go well. When Gail Marie exited Steinmetz's tiny room she was smiling some and crying some.

I called Dwight Wiggens at home as he'd asked me to
do.

"You weren't real truthful with me, Dwight."

He laughed a little. "You can't say that. You never
asked me the right questions, Don. If you had I'd have
answered you truthful."

"Honey and you were very close, I think?"

"Yes. Until her husband came home. I wasn't afraid
of him, but I didn't want any trouble in the club so we
stopped seeing each other then. She called a time or two
and once, after he was home, we got together and
sneaked it." He paused. "Life gets lonely, Don. I wasn't
thinking on marrying her, but I might have done it if
she'd have divorced Stanley and I could have done it
clean."

"I see. I wish you'd have told me."

"It's not something you talk about. How'd you guess
it? We went out of town mostly so no one would see us.
My wife made me promise to her, before she died, that
I'd not chase, not bed someone just for that alone. But,
like I say, life gets lonely. Who told you about us?"

"All the canned food and frozen steaks in her kitchen
told me. Her mother gave her money, but she spent it
on and inside the house. Did you give the food to her?"

"Sure. Out of the club." He paused for a moment.
"And I was here in the club the night she died. I can
prove it."

"I don't doubt it. You're strong enough to have killed
her, but I know you didn't do it because I know who
did."

"Her husband did it," Dwight said confidently.

"No, not him either."

I took Chief George Gentrup, Goldie, and the sheriff from across the river along with me when it was reported to George by that state's officers that Mrs. Milton had returned home. The officers drove their vehicle and stopped before we drew near the ramshackle house. I proceeded on in the darkness in the Toyota truck. They followed on foot.

I parked the Toyota behind an almost new Buick and the Dodge Ram pickup truck with its collection of long guns positioned in the back window.

Lights were on in the house and the land around me smelled of growing things.

I stepped up on the porch and tapped on the door.

An older lady answered and I remembered her, having seen her a few times before at Steinmetz's house. She was small and she had white hair and shrewd eyes. Maybe seventy years old. She was slim and erect and moved well. She was pretty in a doll-like way.

"My name's Robak. I'm a lawyer in practice with Steinmetz, as maybe you'll recall. I've been looking for you for a while."

She smiled genteelly at me. "My Sonny said you were along over here one day asking a lot of questions. What is it you want with me?" She stood in the door and batted at a moth that tried to enter to the light. She peered out into the darkness to see if anyone accompanied me and, when she saw nothing, she smiled.

"I brought you something," I said. "Here's a copy of Steinmetz's old will. It was in effect until this morning." I handed it to her. "In item four you'll note he left you a hundred thousand dollars, all taxes paid."

She batted her eyes at me. "How sweet of him. Did the Judge die this morning then?"

"No. He's doing well. He also wanted me to give you

a copy of his new will which he executed earlier today before some doctors as witnesses. I'm sorry to say he cancelled your bequest."

She appeared flustered. "Why did he do that?"

"He found his daughter. His daughter and others indicated you also looked her up some weeks back in Capitol City. I guess he decided to leave that daughter all his money now that they've found each other. He said to thank you for that."

She clutched both wills to her chest.

"I've one more thing for you. It's Xerox copies of the checks that Judge Steinmetz paid you with for the work you did for him. He thought you might want to show them to a lawyer. He also included, on a separate page, some case law from our state about claims in estates." I handed her that sheaf of papers.

She took them. I could hear movement behind her.

"Sonny," she said softly.

He appeared behind her in the doorway, dwarfing her.

"I have a client across the river who was charged with murdering his wife. I thought for a time that some women might have done the wife in, but then I remembered I'd found birth control pills in her bathroom. So I came over to ask which one of you pair of robbers killed Honey Willetts?"

Sonny laughed and Mrs. Milton smiled.

"I read in the daily paper, over your way, about that," Mrs. Milton said. "Like you just said, her husband's accused of it and the police aren't looking for anyone else."

"He was charged. But today they found some people who can testify that they were with Stanley Willetts at the time his wife died," I lied. "That got them to more checking and they also found some neighbors of Honey Willetts who saw some other things." I gave them both my very best smile. "You'll hear more about it, I'm sure. I found some other stuff that I'm going to take to the sheriff over there tomorrow. But I wanted to bring you up to date on the wills." I waited for a moment. "How much was Sylvia supposed to give you after Gail Marie got the money?"

They said nothing.

"No matter," I said. "My errand's done."

Her voice was hard as steel. "He can cause us a real lot of trouble, Sonny. Let's not let him leave. Get him."

Sonny came around her and out the door swiftly for so large a man. He reached for me and I kicked him in the knee. He grunted and came on and I stepped aside and caught him a decent one on the side of the head. It hurt me more than him. My hand felt as if I'd broken it. He turned back to me.

A voice from the darkness said: "That'll be all, Sonny. Move again and I'll shoot you."

It didn't stop him, but it did slow him. He reached for me once more and I hit him with my good hand in the belly. This time he screamed and bent over and stayed bent.

By the time he straightened up he had three law officers around him, was wearing handcuffs, and the sheriff from his side of the river was reading a search warrant to his mother who was now as white as her hair.

I waited on the porch. A deputy from Bington brought over Mildred Standish and Stanley Willetts, who collectively identified some of Honey Willetts's framed pictures, her camera, and two good antique silver pitchers, all found hidden in the closets of Mrs. Milton's home.

By the time I left, even after Miranda warnings, Sonny Milton and his mother were each blaming the other for Honey's death. He'd done it, but she'd ordered it.

Two months later I took my partner Sam King with me to Capitol City and we went to Jack's Bar. I took Sam with me partly because he was black and mostly because he once had also, on Saturdays in the past, played fine football for good old State U. Then he'd destroyed a knee in a game against Purdue. I thought Jack would enjoy Sam and vice versa.

This time we sat in one of the booths, just Jack and Sam and me. And, after a time of talking eagerly together, Jack and Sam had run out of football for the moment and Sam had gone to the walls to read the newspapers there. I'd already gone over the case some with Jack as he drank his J&B rocks and I drank Canadian and water.

"What's happened to your judge's daughter?" Jack asked.

"They put her in a treatment program. She comes home to Bington on weekends. Maybe it'll work out, maybe not. She has lots of problems. She doesn't remember a lot of what's happened to her over the past years and she's a true addictive personality. But there are plusses that help. Steinmetz doesn't give one single damn about her love life. He told me that people all have sexual trouble and that includes boys with boys, girls with girls, and boys with girls."

"That's the truth," Jack said. He looked me over curiously. "How come you got yourself a black partner? That can't go over too well in ninety-nine percent white Bington. I mean you get outside the university

and they ain't no black people at all around Bington
except when there's a football or basketball game."

"Sam's one hell of a lawyer. We try to keep him
happy. He's a full partner in the firm and he's got lots of
clients. Last year he made, because we have incentives, a
lot more money than I did. And I did very well."

"Okay, I believe you. And you both were saying that
in the search you kind of incidentally found out someone set up another of your clients because of what you
found while looking for the judge's daughter?"

"Yeah. It was some things people said that let me figure it. Honey Willetts, the lady who got killed, had a bit
of taste and smarts, according to her husband and her
mother. Then I find these starving artist twenty dollar
oils on her walls. And some other stuff looked to be
missing, a camera, maybe some other stuff. So someone
took it before, during, or after she died. It would have
been difficult to do before. Honey wouldn't have allowed anything taken from her nest. And the neighbors, or one of them, were watching afterwards. And
that same neighbor said someone left carrying a couple
of heavy boxes the night Honey was beaten to death. So
I figured maybe someone hated Honey and had first
killed her and then stolen from her, maybe to disguise
the reason for the killing. I got lucky looking and found
out who it was who had a real reason to kill Honey. It
got easy for me to figure after Steinmetz told me he
hired Honey as his housekeeper. Jealousy combined
with anger. A lady named Mrs. Milton and her son
went to Honey's house and did her in."

"Tell me about this Mrs. Milton?"

"She worked for Steinmetz until he let her go. Mrs.
Milton didn't care that much about her job loss. Steinmetz had terminated her friendly-like and I'm sure

she'd read the will she found in the house. She therefore was used to the idea of getting a hundred thousand dollars when Steinmetz died, but she liked better the idea of marrying the old man and getting it all. So when she was let go that chance was over. She went first to Capitol City and found Gail Marie. I think she made a deal later, maybe, with Sylvia, but wasn't sure it would work out. So she just couldn't let it end easy. She took Sonny to do the job, but Mrs. Milton probably had to do the background work about knowing Honey's situation and that her burglar husband was home. Or maybe they just lucked into that situation. The sheriff and the state went back to the crime scene afterward, did a fuller check, and found some of Sonny's fingerprints in the house."

"You're into truly interesting work," Jack said. "I'm glad you're alive. I knew Sylvia. She was a mean lady."

"Sure. She was mean because she was mean and not for any other reason. She'd killed some people before."

"When she came in here she drank free," Jack said. "I think you're better than I thought once. And more interesting."

"Life is all interesting," I said as we watched Sam King reading an article about himself. "Tomorrow, for example, I'm going to go to court and get a lady a dissolution of her marriage and also get her an almost new Mercedes she plans to sell."

"Which model?"

"Five hundred series."

"I might find you a buyer for that."

"What's happened to Marta Faye?"

"Never mind her. Let's talk more about this Mercedes and what I can do for you with a buyer."

"Cash?"

He nodded.

And so we did and he did.

And on the day we closed the deal two other things happened. Judy Torpin and Wanda Carson got caught by federal officers taking a cocaine delivery from some crewmen on the *Michael X. Geneva.*

And Stanley Willetts, unable to stand the prosperity of inheriting a house and being out of jail, got caught red-handed in Bington's new Wal-Mart store working in and upon the office safe.

That's how it goes.

Former Circuit Court Judge Joe L. Hensley has written for many magazines, including those in the science fiction and mystery fields. He is the author of a number of novels for the Crime Club, including *Fort's Law* and *Robak's Fire*. This is his ninth novel featuring Don Robak, a lawyer who deals in murder. Hensley lives in Madison, Indiana.